Sally Nicholls

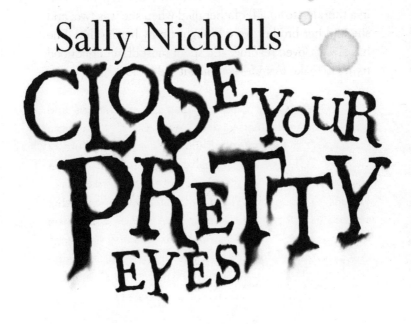

CLOSE YOUR PRETTY EYES

SCHOLASTIC

To my grandparents,
And all other patcher-uppers of families.

First published in the UK in 2013 by Marion Lloyd Books
An imprint of Scholastic Children's Books
Euston House, 24 Eversholt Street
London, NW1 1DB, UK
A division of Scholastic Ltd

Registered office: Westfield Road, Southam Warwickshire, CV47 0RA
SCHOLASTIC and associated logos are trademarks and/or
registered trademarks of Scholastic Inc.

Copyright © Sally Nicholls, 2013

The right of Sally Nicholls to be identified as the author
of this work has been asserted by her.

ISBN 978 1407 12432 2

A CIP catalogue record for this book is available
from the British Library

Printed and bound by CPI Group (UK) Ltd, Croydon, CR0 4YY
Papers used by Scholastic Children's Books are made from
wood grown in sustainable forests.

This is a work of fiction. Names, characters, places,
incidents and dialogues are products of the author's imagination
or are used fictitiously. Any resemblance to actual people,
living or dead, events or locales is entirely coincidental.

1 3 5 7 9 10 8 6 4 2

www.scholastic.co.uk/zone

Praise for Sally N̶

"Exceptional… A terrific story"
Lorna Bradbury, Telegraph

"Absorbing and utterly chilling…"
Bookseller Children's Buyer's Guide

"Writing is a kind of sorcery – and Sally
Nicholls is a true practitioner of the art"
Katy Moran's Book Review Blog

"I love this book"
Jacqueline Wilson

"Elegant, intelligent, moving"
Guardian

"Nicholls is a writer of enormous power
and strength. Wonderful, evocative, lively"
Literary Review

"Absolutely wonderful"
Bookwitch

Sally Nicholls was born in Stockton, just after midnight, in a thunderstorm. Her father died when she was two, and she and her brother were brought up by her mother. She has always loved reading, and spent most of her childhood trying to make real life work like it did in books.

After school, she worked in Japan for six months and travelled around Australia and New Zealand, then came back and did a degree in Philosophy and Literature at Warwick. In her third year, realizing with some panic that she now had to earn a living, she enrolled in a masters in Writing for Young People at Bath Spa. It was here that she wrote her first novel, *Ways to Live Forever*, which won the Waterstone's Children's Book Prize in 2008, and many other awards, both in the UK and abroad. Sally's second novel, *Season of Secrets*, was published in 2009, and her third, *All Fall Down*, in 2012.

www.sallynicholls.com

I think I might be a witch.

Something went wrong when I was born. Other babies got blue eyes and curly hair, but I came out howling and evil. Other babies were sweet and innocent, and their parents loved them, but my mum hated me right from the start.

"I always knew you were a devil," she used to say. "And look how right I was."

Because my mum didn't love me, I had to make other grown-ups like me instead. Right from when I was little, I could make them do what I wanted. I was more powerful than thunder, and I loved it.

But no one ever loved me. I don't suppose anyone ever will. Sometimes people think they do, but that's before they find out what a monster I really am.

THE SIXTEENTH HOME

This is the story of what happened to me the year I was eleven and went to live with the Iveys. You don't have to believe it if you don't want to. Mostly people don't believe me when I tell them things. Mostly they're right not to, because quite often I tell lies, but this time I'm telling the truth. Everything in this story happened like I said it did.

The Iveys were a foster family. Before I came to them I was in this children's home in Bristol called Fairfields, but my ex-foster mother, Liz, thought I'd be better off in a family, and Jim Ivey said he was willing to give me a try. Jim was a friend of Liz's, which was why she asked him to take me. Even after Liz chucked me out for reasons that were totally not my fault, I still saw quite a lot of her. She came to visit me at Fairfields and told me all about Jim, how he lived in this big old house on a farm, with a pig and ducks, and how he was a long-term foster carer, so if we liked each other I could stay until I grew up. I scuffed my feet along the floor when she told me that, and didn't say anything. I've been in foster care on and off since I was a baby, and Fairfields was my fourteenth placement, so I'd stopped believing people when they said I could live with them for ever and ever. I'll tell you about my other so-called homes sometime, and you'll see why.

The Iveys lived outside Bristol, in the proper countryside. It took my social worker, Carole, ages to drive there. At first there were houses and shops, then fields, then fields and hills, then Carole turned the car off the big road on to this little road, which went on for ages along the side of the hill, with hardly any houses or anything. Then she turned off the little road, through a gate and into a farmyard.

"Come on then, cross-patch," she said. I didn't bother replying. Carole was a new social worker. I've had so many over the years, I've lost count.

We got out of the car. I could see:

A long white house, with a green door and windows all with four panes of glass, like a house in a picture book.

A barn with a big door opening on to a big dark space.

A duck pond, with ducks. A yard with chickens.

Carole knocked on the door. A man answered.

Social Services had sent me pictures of the whole family, so I knew who he was. His name was Jim and he was the dad. There wasn't a mum, which was the best thing about the placement as far as I was concerned. Jim was little and wiry and smiley. He wasn't old, exactly, but his hair was beginning to go grey. He had his little girl with him – Harriet, her name was. She was the daughter. She had dark hair and freckles, and she was wearing a red-and-white pirate bandanna, an eyepatch and a plastic hook on one hand.

"I see you've got pirates," said Carole, and Harriet pressed backwards into her dad's legs.

The porch was full of welly boots and footballs. I tried to remember how many kids lived there. I thought it was three and a baby, but it looked like more from the boots. The kitchen was big and old-fashioned. There were kids' pictures all over the walls, and a boy sitting at the kitchen table, drawing. He was Jim's son, Daniel. He was eleven. He smiled at me, then he went back to his picture. I went and looked over his shoulder. It was a pencil drawing of a complicated alien city. Towers and skyscrapers were sticking up into the sky. Spaceships zipped around the towers. Weird alien plants grew out of the pavements.

"Hi," Daniel said, looking up. I didn't say anything.

Jim took Carole and me on a tour of the house, with Harriet trailing behind, still wearing her hook. The house was long and narrow and dark and old.

"It's eighteenth century," said Jim.

There was a dining room, and off it, a little office with a computer. There was a living room with wooden floorboards painted black, rugs, old-fashioned chairs and sofas all different, and bookcases with glass doors, full of old books. All the stuff was tattered-looking, which made

3

me worry, because the worst foster placements were the ones where they wanted you for the money. The house was pretty big though, so they probably weren't *that* poor.

The living room had a real fireplace with a real fire. There was a cat on its back with its stomach turned up to the flames, and a big black girl with a baby sucking on her boob. She was the other foster kid. She glanced at us when we came in, then looked back down at the baby.

"Hey, Grace," said Jim.

Grace grunted.

"This is Olivia, OK? Olivia, this is Grace. She's your new sister. The cat is Zig-Zag. And this little girl is Maisy."

Grace didn't say hello, and neither did I. I've had more sisters and brothers than I can count. The only ones who mean anything are my real sister and brother, Hayley and Jamie. And I haven't seen Jamie since he was a baby, so probably he doesn't count either.

Grace was one of the bad things about the placement. I don't like big kids. The best placements are ones where it's just you, because then the other kids can't hurt you.

My room was up this poky flight of stairs. I hate dark places and I didn't want to go up, but I was afraid Jim might get angry if I didn't, so I had to. The top floor was a long corridor with doors off either side. As you walked along, you had to keep going up a step or down a step, as though whoever built the house had kept changing their mind about how high the floor should be. My room was at the very end of the corridor. It had a bed and a desk and a chest of drawers, but apart from that it was totally bare.

The walls were white, with Blu-tack marks from some other foster kid's posters. There was a clown mug with a couple of chewed-up old pencils on the desk, which made the whole thing look even sadder.

If someone tells you you can stay for ever, then puts you in a room with old Blu-tack marks made by some kid who doesn't live there any more, that tells you everything you need to know.

DANIEL

Jim left me upstairs to unpack, but I didn't. I stayed upstairs for about two seconds, and then I came back down. I hate being on my own. I hate it more than anything. I'd rather be screamed and shouted at than ignored.

There was another staircase at my end of the corridor. It was bigger than the creepy little stairs we'd come up, but not by much. On the landing was a black-and-white photo of an old woman. She looked really old; Victorian or something. She had white hair and wrinkles and she wore a bonnet. She was staring straight into the camera and scowling at me like she hated me. I *definitely* hated her. She looked just like my old foster mother, Violet, who was evil, evil, evil.

Stare all you like, evil woman, I don't care, I thought. But I did care. Just looking at her made me remember horrible things, like what it felt like to be hated, and what it felt like to be small and completely in someone's power. It was as though the woman in the photo was made up of the worst parts of all the worst people I'd ever lived with: my mum, and Violet, and all those temporary homes where they just wanted rid of me as soon as possible.

I could *feel* the hatred coming out of the photograph, and it made me not-at-all-happy about this new family. Why did they have a picture of this woman on their wall? Was she a friend? A relation? Was she going to come and visit? I'd sort of hoped that a friend of Liz's might be OK. But a woman like Violet was a real problem. Could Victorian people still be alive nowadays, or was it too long ago? I moved schools so much, I kept missing the Victorians. I knew they were older than The Beatles, and spitfires, but I wasn't sure if that meant they were all dead. Paul McCartney wasn't.

I went downstairs. Carole and Jim were in the kitchen, drinking tea and talking about me. Harriet was drinking squash.

"Hello, Olivia," said Carole. "Unpacked already? That was quick." I scowled at her. Daniel laughed.

"Dad, can we show Olivia outside?"

"Yeah!" said Harriet. She waved her hook enthusiastically. "Come and meet the pig! And the goats!"

"Go on, then," said Jim.

"I expect I'll be gone when you get back," said Carole. I shrugged.

"Goodbye?" she said. "Thanks for bringing me?"

I gave another shrug. "See you," I said, not looking at her. Then I went out the kitchen door, pushing against her as I passed.

THE GARDEN

I felt better as soon as I was outside. I liked the farmyard. I wondered if there was a tractor. I was pretty sure kids were allowed to drive tractors in farmyards.

"Is your dad a farmer?" I said.

"No," said Daniel. "Well – not really. The fields are all rented out. He's an IT consultant mostly, but not so much at the moment because he looks after Maisy when Grace is in college."

They took me to see the goats. There were two, in a scrubby field with a goat house. The white one was called Morning and the black one was called Night. They had little fluffy beards. They were cool.

The pig was called Pork Scratchings. She had her own fenced-off bit of field, with a low pig house. The field was all churned up and muddy.

"Here, Piggy, Piggy, Piggy," I said, but she didn't come out of her house.

"Come and see the barn," said Daniel.

The barn was dark and musty and smelled of straw. Upstairs, there was a hayloft you could get to by climbing a ladder. Under the hayloft was a whole lot of stuff for foster kids. There were five bikes in different sizes, three scooters, two skateboards, a pedal tractor for toddlers, a pogo stick, some stilts, a unicycle and a real ping-pong table, with bats and balls.

"Can anyone use these?" I said.

"Sure," said Daniel.

I had a go on the pogo stick and the stilts, while Harriet played about on one of the scooters. Daniel rode up and down on the unicycle, showing off.

"Let me have a go!" I said.

"All right," said Daniel. "It's pretty hard, though, at first."

"I'll be fine," I said, but I wasn't. I couldn't even get on the first time I tried, and when I finally did, I fell straight off. Daniel laughed.

"Don't you laugh at me!" I said. "Don't you *dare!*"

"Sorry," said Daniel.

"It is hard," said Harriet. "You've just got to practise."

Like I needed sympathy from an eight-year-old.

"It's stupid," I said. "It's for losers. And clowns. Do I look like a clown?"

Daniel gave me a social-worker look.

"Stop it!" I said. "Stop looking at me like that! I'll kill you!"

"Calm down," said Daniel. "I was only looking."

"No, you weren't!" I kicked the unicycle, hard. "This is rubbish. I had way better stuff than this with my old family."

"Hey." Daniel grabbed the unicycle. "Leave it alone. Just 'cause you can't do it."

He had that expression that everyone starts to wear around me after a while. Hurt. Surprised. Frightened, sometimes, although Daniel didn't look frightened. A little bit angry and a little bit what-did-you-do-that-for? Daniel had only known me ten minutes, and already he didn't like me.

"Stop it!" I shouted. "Stop it right now! Leave me alone!"

"Olivia—" said Daniel. But I spat at him and ran away, before he could follow.

Stupid Daniel, making social-worker faces at me. He didn't even know me. How dare he look at me like that? He was supposed to be my brother. Brothers were supposed to like you. How was I supposed to be nice to him? I was the foster kid. *He* was supposed to be nice to *me*. He wasn't supposed to already hate me ten minutes after he'd met me. The whole fight was *his* fault for looking at me like that.

I was out of the yard by now and behind the house, on a sort of long patio with a low wall. In the middle of the wall were steps, going down into a garden.

The garden was long and wild. It looked like a jungle; an English jungle, with big sprouty plants, and bushes,

11

and trees all tangled with ivy. Once upon a time there would have been a lawn, but now it was covered in long grass, nettles, thistles, and white, naked-looking weeds. Stone things stuck up from the wilderness, broken and abandoned. There was this stone basin in the middle, with purple flowers growing up out of the cracks, and dried up dead things.

It was brilliant.

I picked my way across the wasteland towards the stone thing. It turned out to be a fountain – a proper old dried-up fountain, the sort you get in parks. Behind the fountain was a sort of rockery. I spent a good while jumping from one rock to another, and climbing over the tumbledown walls. I was nearly at the end of the garden now. Behind me was a high wall, and a big tree. Under the tree was some sort of flower bed, although there weren't any flowers: just strong-smelling bushy things and weeds. It was dark, and kind of creepy.

I went closer.

It was even darker under the tree. The earth smelled of plant and cat pee, and something else, strong and unpleasant. The hairs rose on my arms. All of a sudden, I was afraid. It was as though someone was watching me. It frightened me, because I couldn't see where they'd be watching from, unless they were invisible. I looked all around me, and back the way I'd come. No one. Yet I was certain that someone was there. I could *smell* their attention. Someone unfriendly, someone close.

"Hello?"

No answer. But I could *feel* the attention sharpen. It was the feeling you get when you're in a room with someone who hates you. Someone dangerous. I felt like a lion-tamer in a cage with a mad, hungry lion, all crouched down low and ready to pounce. Probably. I've never actually met a lion-tamer, but I bet that was how they'd feel.

I was getting creeped out. *This* was why I didn't like being on my own. I used to feel like this when I broke into other kids' bedrooms in Fairfields – like I was trespassing on someone else's space, someone dangerous, someone who would hurt me if they found me. I turned around slowly, trying to see where someone might be hiding.

There was a noise from behind me. Stones falling, earth breaking. I spun round. But there was no one there.

HOME NUMBER 15

FAIRFIELDS HOME FOR GIRLS

I lived in Fairfields for nearly a year. When they first put me there, I thought that was it. I thought I'd finally gone too far, that they'd all realized how evil I was and now nobody wanted anything more to do with me. I thought I'd never have a family now, and I'd never see Liz, or Hayley, or my mum, or anyone friendly ever again.

I didn't care. I *didn't*. I hated them all. I hated everyone.

Fairfields was a home for girls, and mostly for girls who had been kicked out of foster placements, or run away, or been dumped by other local authorities who wanted to get rid of them. All the staff were trained in restraint, and there was a Quiet Room where you were supposed to go if you were kicking off. They had loads of rules about drugs, and alcohol, and boyfriends, and all this stuff my foster families hadn't even *thought* of.

I was there because:

"We don't have a foster family available with the right set of skills to take you on right now."

Which meant:

"You're a monster. Normal people can't control you."

There were twenty-eight girls in Fairfields when I was there. They were all too messed-up to live in families. They were all bigger than me. And they were all scary. Loads of them drank or used drugs. Loads of them used to run away and live on the streets. One threatened to kill me with a knife. Another told me that if I ever went near her stuff, she'd break into my room and set fire to my bed with me in it. Loads of my stuff got nicked while I was there. Really stupid things, like the trainers Dopey Graham and Grumpy Annabel bought me, which were far too small for the big girls to wear. And precious things, like my necklace with a heart on it that was a present from my sister Hayley.

Fairfields had lots and lots of rules. Rules about not being allowed to ask for seconds until you'd eaten everything on your plate, even if you wanted seconds of sausages and were never ever going to eat your manky beetroot, no matter how hungry you were. Rules about chores and rules about homework. Rules about stupid group therapy sessions, where we all had to sit in a circle and talk about how we felt. Rules about smacking other kids in the face even when they started it and they were bigger than you, and you were only punching them in self-defence anyway.

Some things were OK. There was a big garden. And I had my own room. But mostly I didn't like it. I didn't like the big kids bossing me around. I didn't like the staff, who kept getting new jobs and leaving. It made me tired, getting used to someone and then them just leaving. And I didn't like all the stupid activities, like sport, and making things out of cardboard and paint, and cookery classes. I didn't like that if I was angry or sad or rude, nobody cared, not really.

My other families used to care. Grumpy Annabel, who nearly adopted me, cared when I called her fat and stupid. Liz cared when I had a panic attack in Asda. My first adoptive Mummy and Daddy cared when I screamed and screamed and wouldn't shut up. Here, no one minded. I was just one of lots of kids and their shift finished at ten and they went home to their real children, who were well-behaved and clever and loved them.

At Fairfields, I used to worry all the time about disappearing. About what would happen if I didn't come home from school, or just vanished, if anyone would even notice. I felt like I was slipping away, all the time. I started doing that thing I used to do when I lived with Violet, where my body would be in the TV room, but my head would be floating somewhere else. Sometimes I'd float over my body. Sometimes I'd still be there, but I'd stop feeling anything. I had to be careful, though. Sometimes it would go wrong and I'd be back standing in the cold shower at Violet's, or getting smacked into the wall by my mum, or having cigarettes burnt into my arm. I could never escape, not really.

I was scared a lot of the time at Fairfields. I was scared that the big girls would break into my room at night and suffocate me with a pillow. I used to start crying for no reason at all. I started getting nightmares again, and I used to wet the bed too. The care workers didn't mind, but I always hated it.

Liz came to visit me a couple of times. The first time I screamed and screamed and wouldn't let her into the room. The second time I threw my remote control at her and told her that I hoped she got eaten by werewolves. Both times she just turned straight around and left. But she kept coming back. And the third time I let her stay.

"I still hate you," I told her. "I still think you're a liar and a loser."

Liz got up like she was about to go and I felt like I was choking, like I was dying, like everyone I ever loved was always going to leave me.

"Don't—" I said. It came out of my mouth without me even realizing it. Liz stopped.

"Come on, love," she said, and she gave me a hug. I liked it at first, but then I stopped liking it and pulled away.

She took me to the park. I didn't have much stuff left by that point. Some of it had got nicked, or smashed, and some I'd grown out of, or had to leave behind. But I still had the skateboard that Dopey Graham and Grumpy Annabel had bought me. Liz let me play for ages on the skateboard ramps, then she bought me chips with lots of ketchup at the park café.

17

"Are you coming next week?" I said, and she looked a bit sad.

"I'd like to," she said. "I'm hoping my new lad will be seeing his grandparents on Saturdays, but I'll have to see what happens."

She had some other kid now. Some kid she liked more than me. Another kid sleeping in my room, in my bed, playing with the bike and the trampoline and the Xbox, eating her banana custard. I thought of all the hundreds and hundreds of foster kids she'd probably had, and how stupid I was to think she'd liked me especially.

I hated her. I *hated* her. I felt like she'd tricked me. She'd made me think she liked me, when really I was just another foster kid like all the rest.

USUALLY I'M WORSE

I was expecting Jim to tell me off when I got back to the house. I was sort of dreading it, but sort of interested too. I wanted to know what sort of dad he was going to be.

He was in the kitchen, washing up. He looked around when I came in.

Uh-oh.

I burst out talking before he could start.

"What are you doing? Are you washing up? Can I help? I like washing up. I'm ever so good at it. Can I dry? Can I put away?"

"Calm down." Jim smiled at me. "Where did you get to? We thought you'd run away."

"I went for a walk," I said. "Can I help, then?"

"Yes, you can," said Jim. "But not right now. For now

I'd like you kids to get to know each other. Why don't you go and say hello to Grace?"

He didn't say it in a mean way. He was smiling, but it didn't exactly make me feel welcomed.

Jim put his hand on my shoulder and led me into the living room. Grace, the big girl with the baby, was still there. Baby Maisy was asleep in her lap and Grace was reading this big book over her head.

I went and stood in front of her. She ignored me.

"There you go," said Jim. "Grace, can you keep an eye on Olivia for a minute?"

And he went.

Grace didn't look up from her book. She didn't even *grunt*.

I'm worth at least a grunt.

I waited for her to say something. She didn't. I hate being ignored. I hate it worst of *anything*.

"Can I play with your baby?" I said.

"No," said Grace. "She's asleep."

"I could wake her up. I'm dead good at babies. I've got this baby brother, and I know how to feed him and stop him crying and *everything*."

Grace sort of grunted and turned the page. I came closer.

"What book are you reading? Is it good? I've read hundreds of books. My old mum and dad used to buy me loads when I lived with them. I've got all the Horrible Histories, and *Horrid Henry,* and all the Harry Potter books. I bet I've read that book you're reading."

That was a bit of a lie. I *did* used to own those books, but I didn't read them. Most of the time, I used to tear them to bits to annoy my old mum, Grumpy Annabel. She and my old dad used to spend a fortune on books for me, and it narked her off no end when I tore them to shreds.

Grace tipped her book up so I could see the cover.

"*Oliver Twist*. Isn't that a film?"

Grace put down the book. Result!

"Are you being deliberately idiotic?" she said.

I grinned at her. "Me? You're the one reading a big, stupid, boring old book. Why are you doing that, anyway?"

"Because."

"Because why?"

"Because I like it. Because I need to read it for my English A Level. Because I need to get all As in my A Levels, and probably A*s, so I can go off to university and never have to talk to ridiculous little kids like you for the rest of my life." She stuck the book up over her face and turned the page, very deliberately.

"Can babies go to university?" I said.

"Aargh!" Grace flung down the book. "Yes, of course they can! They get top marks in crapping and dribbling!"

I giggled. Grace gave me an evil look.

"Are you always this annoying?" she said.

"Are you always this grumpy?"

"No," said Grace. "Usually I'm worse."

NIGHT

Some houses have proper strict bedtimes and some don't. Jim's did. Maisy went to bed first, then Harriet, then Daniel and me. I don't know if Grace had a bedtime or not, but probably not because she was nearly grown-up.

I didn't want to go to bed, but I did anyway. It's usually a good idea to be well-behaved with new people, in case they turn out to be secretly evil. I was pretty worried when Jim left, though. I hate the first night in a new place. *Anyone* could come in and do *anything* to you. If I was a foster parent, I'd put locks on all my kids' doors, so no one could get in. But they never do.

"Sleep tight," said Jim, and he left me.

I lay there in the dark, listening to the *creak creak creak* of his feet in the corridor. As soon as he'd gone downstairs, I got out of bed and turned the light back on.

I lay on my back and listened. These are the things I could hear:

"All I Need Is a Miracle" playing on the kitchen radio.

Jim talking to Grace about me.

The walls going *creak creak creak*.

Harriet turning over in bed.

The wind blowing around the house, trying to get in.

A tree *rhooshing* as the wind lifted it up and all its leaves rustled.

A dog barking.

An owl going *hoohoo* somewhere in the night.

Something – mice, maybe – scratching in the walls.

A fly buzzing against the windowpane in the bedroom next door.

Something else *tap-tap-tap*-tapping at my window.

A *creak* – was someone coming upstairs? No, just Jim shutting the kitchen door.

I have superpowers. I've had them for as long as I can remember. I have supersonic hearing and a super sense of smell. I hear things other people don't – tiny noises, scratchings, creakings, whispers. I hear foster parents telling each other they can't cope with me any more. I hear other kids rifling through my stuff downstairs, and my mum opening a can of cider at the other end of the flat. I can tell just by the way a person is standing what they think of me. My therapist, Helen, says they aren't really superpowers. She says I can do these things because of the bad things that happened to me when I was little. She says because my body is so worried about being hurt, it pays attention to *everything*, pretty much *always*. Other people mostly just pay that much attention when they're somewhere scary, but I do it all the time because when I was little and lived with my mum, I was always afraid.

These are the things I could smell from my bed:

Cold air from the half-open window.

Dust, and bare wood from my wooden floor.

Fairfields shampoo in my hair.

Soft, dry hair smell.

Clean sheets.

Hairs from Daniel's cat, Zig-Zag.

Wet-leaved ivy-smell from outside.

Lavender from the paper in my new chest of drawers.

Tomato-and-onion-and-mushroom smell, drifting up the stairs from dinner.

None of it felt familiar. None of it felt safe. Some of it felt very *unsafe*. That tapping at the window. I knew it was just a branch or something, but it freaked me out. I'd be lying there, trying to sleep, and I'd just be drifting away when I'd hear it again.

Tap tap tap.

I'd jerk awake, stiffening. What was that? Oh. That tree. I'd lie there, listening, waiting to hear it again. *Was it just a tree branch? What if it was something else?* Someone's fingers, someone tall, someone on a ladder. I knew it wasn't that really. But it didn't stop me being afraid. I hate sleeping in a room with an open window, because I'm always afraid of what might climb through. I wanted to go and shut it, but I was too scared of whatever was making the tapping.

When I lived with Violet, I shared a room with this girl who used to come and put a pillow over my head at night.

"Think you're hard, do you?" she'd say. "How'd you like this, then?" And she'd hold the pillow there while I struggled and choked. She never held it on for long, but she would have done, if she'd felt like it. If she'd been angry or crazy enough, one night, she would have killed me. I've lived with lots of girls like that. Perhaps Grace was a girl like that too.

And then there was Jim. I didn't know Jim and I didn't trust him. That first night in the Iveys' house, I didn't sleep at all.

HOW NOT TO BE LONELY

The next day, there was school.

I've been to a lot of schools. Big schools. Little schools. Schools where you do music and dance and drama and football. Schools where they don't notice if you don't turn up for weeks. I've been to schools where I had some lady following me around all the time, correcting my spelling and telling me to behave, and schools where most of the kids didn't speak English. I've been to schools where everyone was terrified of me, and schools where I was terrified of *everyone*.

This school was OK. A new school is easier to understand than a new house, though the rules do change. My new school was in Tollford, which was a boring little town with cobbled streets and souvenir shops. Grace went to school too: sixth-form college, in a taxi paid for by Social Services. Maisy stayed at home with Jim. She had a playpen in his study, so he could work while she was playing, though I don't know how much work he really did. Babies need lots of playing with.

None of the kids in my class liked me, I could tell. Some of the grown-ups did. (They didn't know me yet.) Daniel went to the same school, but he was in a different class. I'd never been to a school with two year-six classes before. Harriet was three years below. Neither of them wanted to talk to me at break, though. I knew they wouldn't. They had their own friends. Daniel just went off and played football with the other boys.

I didn't care. I went and joined in. I got a good few kicks in too, before they stopped me.

"What are you doing? No one said you could play!"

"You were in the middle of a game!" I said.

"You don't even have a team," said another kid. He looked furious.

"I'm on my brother's team," I said, which confused them all no end.

"You don't have a brother."

"Yes, I do," I said. "Daniel's my brother."

Everyone looked at Daniel, who went red.

"Well, yes, she's my sister. Sort of." He saw me glaring at him and said, "I mean, yes, she's my sister. Come on, let her play, she's only new."

So that was all right.

"Why don't you play with your own friends?" Daniel

said, on the way home. "The girls in your class, why don't you play with them?"

Because the other girls in my class were losers. And they all had their own friends already. If Daniel didn't let me play football, I wouldn't have anyone.

"You're my friend," I said. "Aren't you?"

"I guess so," said Daniel.

But he didn't look that sure.

People never like me. Mostly, they like me when they first meet me, and then when they get to know me they stop. Most grown-ups, anyway. Plenty of kids just never like me ever. It makes me want to not bother making friends, because what's the point when they're just going to dump me? And even if they magically *don't* dump me, I usually have to leave anyway. I'm *always* having to leave. You'd think I'd be used to it, but I'm not. Every time it happens I try and get used to it, but I never do.

Really what I should do is just not bother liking anybody ever, but it's hard not liking anyone. It's *lonely*. It's especially lonely if you don't have a mum and dad, because then you don't have anybody, and not having anybody is the worst feeling in the whole world. I think I'd rather be dead than not have anybody, which is why I always try and make new people like me, because then I have someone for a little bit, which is better than nobody at all. But I try not to like people too much, because the more you like someone, the harder it is at the end, when you have to go.

The more I got to know Daniel, the more I liked him. I didn't want to, but I couldn't help it. I thought when I first met him he was going to be totally goody-goody and boring. Harriet was like that a bit, but he wasn't. The first week I was there, we were playing on our bikes in the yard. Daniel and I were showing off what tricks we could do – wheelies and spins and jumps, and stuff off the packing cases.

"When I was at Fairfields," I said, "there was this kid who rode her bike off the garage roof."

"Did she die?" said Daniel, hopefully.

"No! At least, I don't think so. It was before I lived there."

"I bet she didn't do it really," Daniel said. "You'd die if you rode a bike off a roof."

"You wouldn't!" I said. "Not if you landed on your wheels, you wouldn't."

"You wouldn't land on your wheels," said Daniel.

"*I* would!" I said.

So then, of course, I had to do it.

I wanted to ride off the actual barn roof, but it turns out it's pretty hard to get a bike up a ladder, even with Daniel holding on to the bottom. In the end, we dragged the bike up the stairs to the hayloft at the top of the barn. The hayloft was a bit of a stupid name, because when the farmer who rented Jim's fields actually brought in the hay – later in the summer – it went underneath, by the ping-pong table and the bikes.

"You aren't really going to do it, are you?" said Harriet.

Harriet was a bit wet, but I liked having her there to look impressed. What's the point of riding a bike off a hayloft if you don't have anyone to look impressed?

"Course I am," I said. I wasn't worried. I was scared of the things other people might do to me, but the things I did to myself – climbing too high up trees, riding my bike too fast down hills, walking all the way along the top of the roof at Fairfields – that sort of stuff never bothered me. I broke my arm when I was seven, falling out of a tree, and I never even cried.

My plan was to sort of spin in the air and then land on my wheels. It didn't quite work though. I lifted the front wheel up when I rode off the edge of the loft, thinking I'd leap up, like you do when you jump, but I just went down, and a lot quicker than I'd expected. I didn't have time to spin or anything. I went from in the air to on the ground in about two seconds flat.

Harriet started screaming. "Olivia! Are you dead? Are you dead?"

"Of course I'm not," I said. And I wasn't. I tore a great hole in my jeans though, and a big raggedy patch on the sleeve of my jacket. My leg and my arm were both pouring blood. That was why Harriet screamed, all that blood. I didn't scream.

"Doesn't it hurt?" said Daniel, but it didn't, not really. One of my superpowers is not really feeling pain – or hot – or cold – or hungry. I just don't notice things like that the way ordinary people do. I *can* feel hurt, but my arm has to be practically falling off before I do. My stupid

30

therapist, Helen, says it's because I got hurt so often when I was little. She thinks it's a bad thing, because it means I keep forgetting to wear a coat when it's cold, or don't notice when I've hurt myself. *I* think she should try living in a children's home for a week and *then* tell me it's a crappy superpower.

I thought Jim would be angry with me for riding off the loft, but he wasn't.

"It's your arm, mad woman," he said, which I liked. It was the sort of thing Liz would have said. I hoped I might have to go to hospital, but Jim just washed all the gravel out of my arm and leg and stuck the whole thing over with big plasters.

"You're bonkers, Olivia Glass," said Daniel, but I could tell he liked it, just a little bit.

"I'll ride off the house roof next," I said.

HOME NUMBER 14

SARAH AND TONY

Before I lived in Fairfields, I was with this couple called Sarah and Tony. I moved in with them after Liz told me I couldn't live with her any more.

I didn't understand at first.

"But *why* do I have to go?" I said. "I've been so good."

Usually when people move me, it's because I've been bad. But for Liz I was really, really good. I thought Liz was wonderful. And I thought she liked me too.

Ha.

"Olivia," said Liz. She knelt down next to me and looked into my eyes. I squirmed away. "Listen, I've loved having you live with me. You know that. But this was always a temporary placement. The plan was always that you'd stay with me for a year and a half, and then we'd find a new family for you."

"But *why*?" I said. I still didn't get it. I wanted to live with Liz, and Liz was the first person in years who'd loved having me live with her. I did know it was only supposed to be temporary, but if Liz really loved me, like she said she did, that wouldn't matter, would it? A real mum would want to keep me for ever, wouldn't she?

"Olivia, this is my job," said Liz. "I look after young people and help them learn how to live in a family. And then when my job's done, my kids are able to go out and live with someone new. If I kept all the kids who've lived here, I'd need a house as big as Hogwarts."

She was trying to make me laugh, but it didn't work.

"You only like me because they *pay* you," I said. "You're a big liar and I *hate* you!"

"You live with me because that's my job," said Liz. "But that's not why I like you. I like you because I like you. And I hope your new family will like you too, and you'll be able to stay there until you're grown up."

She was a stinky liar pants. No family was ever going to keep me. She was a big, fat, stupid, ugly, horrible, nasty liar.

"I'm going to kill them!" I told Liz. "Whoever they put me with. I'm going to rip out their eyes and feed them to toads. I'm going to break everything they own into a million, billion, trillion pieces!"

"Mm-mm," said Liz. She did that when I said things she didn't like. Pretended she couldn't hear me until I said something nice.

"I'll kill you too!" I said, and I punched her as hard as I could in the stomach.

33

"Olivia, go to your room," said Liz.

"I won't!" I said, and I punched her again. She doubled over, and suddenly I was afraid. I thought Liz was so powerful, I thought she could protect me from everything, but I could just punch her and she couldn't do anything about it.

She walked out of the room and called Social Services, and I moved out the next day.

I knew I was going to hate the people I moved in with, Sarah and Tony. My bedroom was yucky pink. The other foster kids were these big boys who frightened me. And the first night I was there, Sarah served pasta sauce that looked like sick. I told her I wasn't going to eat it and she said, "All the more for the rest of us then," which is just what Liz used to say. I was so angry, I threw my glass of water at her, and she said, "None of that, kiddo," and locked me in the bathroom. I was furious. I was furious with Sarah and Tony for not being Liz, and furious with Liz for not wanting to keep me, and furious with myself for not being the sort of kid she'd want to keep. I kicked a great big hole in the door, and I smashed the medicine cabinet with my elbow, so there was glass all over the floor. I picked up this bit of broken glass and stabbed it into my arm, over and over and over again until the blood gushed out and over the floor, just to feel something that wasn't this.

Sarah said she didn't want me after that, and I got sent to Fairfields.

TWO THINGS HAPPENED TO ME ON FRIDAY

The Friday after I came to live with the Iveys, two things happened.

The first thing was, Liz rang.

"Hello, love," she said. "How's it going?"

"Fine," I said. "Absolutely fine. Actually, I'm really busy now, so I'll probably have to go and do that thing I was really busy doing. Sorry!"

"What were you doing?" said Liz. I could hear her almost laughing at me down the phone, which made me angry and also sort of happy, that she knew me well enough not to get pissed off when I pretended I didn't want to talk to her.

"I'm playing on my new bike," I said. "And my new skateboard, and my new unicycle, which Daniel taught me how to use and now I can ride it even better than he can, and *I* can do juggling at the same time, only I drop the balls sometimes."

That bit wasn't actually true, but it wasn't like Liz would ever find out.

"You and Daniel are getting on then?" said Liz.

"Oh, yeah," I said. "Daniel and me are best friends."

"I like Daniel," said Liz, and my stomach tightened, because everyone likes nice kids better than me.

"You all set for tomorrow?" she said. She was supposed to be coming to see me. I wasn't sure if I wanted to see her, though. Not if she liked Daniel more than me.

"Dunno," I said. "Because, actually, I'm going to be doing tricks on a unicycle tomorrow, so I might be too busy."

"That's a shame," said Liz. "I've cleared all this time off so I can come and visit."

I hesitated. "Really cleared time off?" I said.

"Really, really," said Liz.

Silence.

"Though I could always go to the *Doctor Who* meet-up instead," said Liz. Liz was a massive *Doctor Who* fan. She had pictures of Daleks stuck up all over her kitchen, and an air freshener shaped like a TARDIS that let out a nice smell when you spun it through time and space. She had a cyberman costume in her garage that she used to dress up in for conventions.

"I don't care," I said.

"See you at half eleven, then?" said Liz.

"Yeah," I said. "Only not half eleven. Come at half

one, 'cause I've got lots of important things that I need to be doing tomorrow morning."

Liz laughed, in a way that made my heart clench.

"OK, sweetheart," she said. "Half past one."

And then there was the other thing.

I was coming down the creepy servants' stairs when I heard this noise. It was a baby crying, upstairs somewhere, on and on and on.

It gave me the shivers. I hate babies' crying. I always have. And this baby sounded so lonely and sad. It sounded like a baby who nobody loved, who nobody cared for. Which was frightening, because of course it must be Maisy, and if Jim could hear Maisy crying like that and not do anything about it, then he wasn't as nice as he'd been pretending to be.

I stood on the stairs, listening to the baby and getting more and more afraid. But I couldn't stay halfway up for ever, so I didn't. I went down.

Grace was in the living room, reading another big, boring book. Maisy was on the floor, playing with her wooden bricks. She wasn't crying at all. She was laughing.

Which just made me even more afraid.

Because if it wasn't Maisy crying, then who was it?

I don't do very well when I'm scared. Mostly what happens is, I get angry. I get angry a lot.

I went into the dining room. Jim was sitting by the fireplace with Zig-Zag on his lap, reading a letter.

"There's a baby crying," I told him. He looked a bit surprised.

"Maisy's crying?" he said. "Is she? I can't hear anything."

"*No*," I said. "It's not Maisy. It's another baby. A baby who isn't there!"

"Oh," said Jim. "Well, that's good. I wouldn't want to think that a real baby was crying."

He was laughing at me. He thought I was just being stupid.

"It's not funny!" I yelled. "Stop it!" I grabbed his letter out of his hands and tore it up. It served him right. He was treating *my* important things like rubbish. It served him right if I did the same to him.

Jim didn't agree though. He made me do all the washing-up as punishment. People always blame me for everything.

THERAPY

I had therapy when I lived at Fairfields. It was a waste of time. My therapist was this idiot woman called Helen who kept asking me questions like, "How did you feel about that?" or "Why did you do that, then?"

I used to turn it into a game. I would pretend to be this sweet little orphan and blink at her and tell her how sad I was because the other kids used to pick on me. I'd tell her everything mean the other kids did, and everything mean the workers did, and hope she'd leave me alone.

She was pretty stupid though. She kept asking me stupid questions, about Liz, and my old adoptive parents, Grumpy Annabel and Dopey Graham, and all sorts of things I'd made it perfectly clear I didn't *want* to talk about.

"How do you feel about not living with Liz any more?" she'd say, and I'd shrug.

"Fine."

"Really?" she'd say. "How did you feel when she told you?" And I'd shrug again.

"Still fine."

Sometimes she'd just sit there and not say anything and wait for me to talk. I hated that even more. I used to make stuff up. I'd tell her I was afraid of ghosts, or monsters under the bed, or some other rubbish. I'd start fights with her.

"Why are you telling me off when you're the fat, ugly one? Why don't you lose some weight and get some plastic surgery before you start picking on me?"

Disagreeing with whatever she said was also good.

"You sound very angry."

"No, I'm not."

"How do you feel then?"

"Fine."

"What would you like to happen now?"

"Doughnuts. Jam doughnuts. And laser death rays."

"Does acting like this make you feel safe?"

"Not as much as laser death rays would."

She wouldn't shut up though.

If she'd really wanted to help, she could at least have given me the doughnuts.

I thought I'd get out of going to therapy once I came to live with the Iveys, but no such luck. Some lunatic was paying for a taxi to take me there every Monday after school.

"But it's pointless!" I wailed, when Liz told me.

"Of course it's pointless if you never do anything!" said Liz. "Honestly. How exactly do you think Helen is going to help you if you just sit there and glare at her? Get working, kid. You're not stopping until you do."

This was just another example of bonkers grown-up logic. Something doesn't work, so you keep doing it until it starts to. If Liz *really* wanted me to be happy, there were loads of things she could do about it. Doughnuts would be a good start, but I wouldn't say no to lasers.

TWO WOMEN

Liz came to visit on Saturday. I wasn't exactly sure how I felt about it. I liked Liz, but I was still angry with her.

When I saw her, though, I was pretty pleased. She looked just the same as always – little, with red shoes, black curly hair that was starting to go grey, and a round face which was always laughing. Liz was about the most cheerful person I knew. It was nearly impossible to piss her off, and I should know. I tried really hard when I lived with her.

She put her arm around me and gave me this massive hug and said, "How're you doing, sport?"

I hate all that "How are you?" stuff, so I mumbled, "I'm OK." I didn't want to talk about me any more, so I said, "Did you know Jim's got ducks? There are six of them and they've all got names. Daniel and Harriet named them, but I said it wasn't fair that they named them all and I didn't, so Harriet said I could name two of them. Come and see—" And I dragged on her arm to pull her over.

"Hey!" Liz pulled her arm away. "What do you do if you want to ask me something?"

"Ugh!" Liz was awful about rules. "One day I'm going to be drowning," I told her, "and I'll be yelling, 'Save me! Save me!' and you'll be all, 'That's not an appropriate way to ask for help,' but by then I'll be *dead* and—"

"Yep," said Liz. "I'm a cold-hearted woman, I am. So you'd better practise asking properly, hadn't you? Otherwise the fishes'll be feeding on Olivia and chips."

"Huh," I said. "You wouldn't care. You'd be *happy* if I drowned, then you wouldn't have to keep coming to visit."

"Yep," said Liz. "Must be tough, having this horrible old woman who loves you so much."

"You don't love me!" I said. "You don't love me *at all!*"

"Too right," said Liz. And she grabbed me and started tickling me. I squealed.

"Stop it! Let me go!"

"Who's come to visit you because she loves you? Who?"

I wouldn't say it.

"I don't know!" I said. "No one!" But Liz wouldn't stop. "OK, you! You! Stop it!"

"Damn right I love you," said Liz. "Let's go, shall we?"

We went to Bristol, because I said I was fed up of fields. We went to the cinema and then for a walk by the canal.

We counted canal boats and fed the ducks, and admired the little baby ducklings all following their mother in a line. Then we had scampi and chips at a pub and watched the canal boat people opening and closing the locks to let the narrowboats through.

"I wish I lived in a narrowboat," I said, but Liz said she didn't.

"Spiders," she said. "And damp."

But I wouldn't care. I'd just like to be somewhere where no one could mess with my stuff, and no one could make me do anything I didn't want to, because if they tried, I'd just motor off, and no one would ever find me.

"But what about me?" said Liz. "If I wanted to visit you, how would I know where to come?"

"You wouldn't," I said. "I'd be gone."

I had a pretty good time with Liz. It's *tiring* living with strangers, always trying to be nice in case they realize how horrible you are really and go off you. I hadn't realized quite how tiring it was until I had an afternoon off.

It was nearly seven when we got home. Tea was bubbling on the hob and Jim told me to "run and put your things upstairs – quick."

I would have gone round and up the bigger stairs at the other end of the house, but everyone was looking at me, so I had to go up the little creepy servants' stairs, round the corner where nobody could see me, on to the landing where anyone could be waiting to leap out and grab me, and—

There was someone there.

It was a woman. I was absolutely sure of it. I could *smell* her, this weird old-lady, dry-skin, alcohol-and-tobacco-smell, with coal-smoke, and milk, and something medicine-y behind it. Whoever she was, she was close.

I froze. Was it my mum? Was it Violet? Could they have found me? My mum *did* used to say she'd come and find us in our foster homes. She never did it, but this time maybe she had?

I stayed absolutely still, straining to hear her. She didn't smell like Violet, and she smelled older than my mum. I waited. There were footsteps coming down the upstairs corridor towards me but I was too scared to move in case she heard me.

I was in the landing space, hidden from anyone looking up from downstairs. I was completely alone.

And suddenly I was swept over with that same feeling I'd had when I'd first seen the photograph of the Victorian woman on the landing. A feeling of being small, and alone, and powerless, and living in the house of someone who wanted me to suffer. It made me want to cry, but I was too terrified to make a noise. I just stood there, as the footsteps came closer. Whoever it was came down the corridor, and then the stairs began to creak, as though someone was walking down them towards me. But there was nobody there. The footsteps were empty.

I tried to open my mouth to scream, but I couldn't.

There's a thing I do when I'm afraid. I took myself out

of that place. My body didn't move, but I hid my mind somewhere far away, somewhere safe.

When I came back, the woman was gone.

HOME NUMBER 13

LIZ

Liz was what is called a specialist placement. The idea was that I was supposed to live with her for a year and a half, and she was going to teach me how to be a good little girl, and then I'd be all ready to go and be perfect in some other family.

I moved in with her after my second set of adoptive parents, Dopey Graham and Grumpy Annabel, gave me the boot. I don't blame Graham and Annabel for dumping me. I was pretty horrible to them. I broke all Grumpy Annabel's ornaments, and I pissed in her bed, and I threw plates at her, and told her lies, and broke all the toys they gave me, and kicked and bit and hit her. I was surprised they kept me for so long actually. If I'd been my kid, I'd have chucked me in the dustbin months ago. But they were both kind of idiots.

Dopey Graham was practically crying when he dropped me off.

"You know we still love you, sweetheart," he said. "You'll always be our little girl, whatever happens."

"Yeah, whatever," I said. "Can't you go now?"

Dopey Graham looked like I'd punched him.

"Aren't you going to miss us?" he said. "Your own mummy and daddy?"

"You're not my daddy," I told him. "And she's not my mummy. And I never want to see either of you again!"

"Princess. . ." said Dopey Graham, and then he did start to cry, but I spat at him and ran into the house, where I didn't have to see him. He and Grumpy Annabel were just like the first set of idiots who wanted to adopt me. They kept saying how much they loved me, but I knew they'd chuck me out in the end. I just *knew* it.

I didn't want to go and live with Liz at first. She was a lady living on her own, and they were always the worst. Violet was a lady on her own, and so was my mum. Also, all the social workers kept going on about how she was going to make me behave and how "you won't be able to try any of your tricks with her," so I figured she was probably going to beat me up. I knew from living with Violet and my mum how women made you behave. Cigarette burns, and hitting you, and locking you in the cellar. Not that it ever worked. I was still just as bad with them as I always was.

Living with Liz was . . . interesting, though. She wasn't anything like I'd expected. When I told her, "I wish you

48

were dead! I hate you!" she didn't get angry like my other foster mums did. She just laughed and gave me a hug and said, "Well, I love you!" like she really meant it.

It was really, really hard to get her angry. Like, the first day I was there, I told her I wasn't going to eat her stupid food, and she just laughed and said, "All the more for me, then!" and carried on munching happily while I sat there feeling like a fool.

"What am I going to eat?" I said eventually, and she said, "How about breakfast?"

If I screamed and threw a fit, she just went and worked in her garden. Once, I followed her outside and started pulling up her plants, and she went straight back inside and locked the door. I pulled up all the vegetables in the garden and stamped on them, and threw the dirt at her window. She left me out there for ages, until it got dark and I got tired of stamping on things. Then, when I was quiet, she let me in and gave me a big bowl of porridge.

"Aren't you angry?" I asked. Usually it drove people mad when I broke their stuff. It used to scare my old adoptive mother, Grumpy Annabel. I was eight when I stopped living with her, but I used to scare her all the time.

"I've been watching *Match of the Day*," said Liz. "I've had a lovely evening." And I felt tired and sad and lonelier than ever. She didn't care about me. She didn't care that I'd been out there all evening in the cold.

"Maybe next time you can watch too," she said, and she gave me a hug. I wriggled away.

"I broke all your stupid plants," I told her.

"I know," she said. "We'll need to do something about that tomorrow."

In my other homes, I could get away with anything, and nobody could punish me. If they told me to say "sorry" or go to my room, I wouldn't. My first set of adoptive parents got scared of trying to punish me because I used to get so angry when they tried. I used to kick their kid and smash holes in their walls, and in the end they decided it was less hassle not to tell me off. Liz didn't tell me off either, but she did make me pay. I had to replant her vegetables – all the ones which weren't dead, anyway – and pay for the ones I'd destroyed by doing stuff for her, like hoovering and mopping and loading the dishwasher.

"I won't!" I told her the first time. She just handed me a spade and a pair of gardening gloves and smiled.

"Take as long as you want, pet," she said. "I'll be inside. I might make some fairy cakes."

And she just left me there. I stuck my tongue out at her. If she thought I was going to do her stupid gardening, she had another think coming.

Instead of gardening, I made myself a den in her hedge. I built a roof from old tarpaulin, and dragged in the birdbath for a table. I wrote

PRIVATE
OLIVIA'S HOUSE
DEATH TO ALL INVADERS

with little pebbles on the earth. It took ages, but I sort of enjoyed it. I pretended it was my house, and I was going to stay there for ever and ever and ever, and make Liz be my slave.

It was a nice pretend, but it got a bit boring by lunchtime. I thought maybe Liz wouldn't give me any food, because I'd been bad, but she did. Chicken soup and bread with lots of cheese. She'd made a whole tray of fairy cakes too.

"Are they for me?" I asked.

"Of course, love," she said. "We'll have some when you've finished the garden."

She wasn't going to give up on that stupid garden. I slumped further down in my chair.

"It's too *hard*," I whined, in the baby voice that always worked on my old adoptive father, Dopey Graham. It didn't work on Liz, though.

"Off you go!" she said, cheerfully. She was always bloody cheerful.

I trudged into the garden. *I'm not going to do her stupid work*, I thought, but somehow the fun had gone out of the fight. It started to get cold. Liz turned the living-room light on, and I could see her in the living room doing something with paper and glitter and card. It looked fun.

I sat there dribbling earth through my fingers all afternoon. Liz came to fetch me at teatime.

"I'm not digging your stupid garden," I told her.

"That's OK, pet," she said, and she gave me another hug. "There's always tomorrow."

51

She never gave up. In the end, you just got bored and did whatever it was she wanted.

In most of my other homes, I got to be boss. Liz never let me be boss. In my other homes, it was a big fight.

"You will do what I tell you!"

"No, I won't!"

The families where I didn't get to be boss were the ones with people like Violet, who made you stand in a cold shower if you didn't do as you were told, or put you in the cellar. Liz didn't do that. But she always made me fix whatever mess I made. And if I was rude to someone, I had to pay them back by doing something nice.

"But I'm not sorry!" I said, after I called that day's new social worker a lazy fat cow. "She *is* a lazy fat cow."

"No arguing," said Liz. She never let me argue. "You're rude to someone, you make up for it." And I had to make a SORRY card for the fat cow and send it off to her. Huh.

It was scary not being the boss. But it was also nice, because it was hard work being in charge, and sometimes – maybe for half an hour or so – I could forget that I had to be, and I liked that.

The other thing Liz did was, she never said I was wonderful or lovely or beautiful, like some of my other families did. But she was always setting sneaky traps to make me do stuff, and then she'd go, "Nice work, Olivia," or "Well done!"

I was never sure how I felt about that. Part of me would be pleased, like, *I did something good*. But the rest of me felt weird, because I'm *not* someone good, so when she said I was, it was like I didn't know who I was, and I hated that. I didn't like being evil, but at least I knew who I was when I was horrible.

So after she'd told me that, sometimes I'd go and do something really bad, like break all her plates, *smash smash smash*, or call her a stupid bitch.

"Do you *like* doing bad things?" Liz asked me, once.

I gave a sort of shrug. Of course I didn't like it. But it was who I was.

"Do you *like* getting so angry?" she said, and I shrugged again.

"It's what I do," I said.

"It doesn't have to be," said Liz. But I never believed her.

I felt safer living with Liz than I've felt since I can't remember when. I always had to be on my guard when I lived with people like Dopey Graham, because I knew if anyone came to do anything bad to me, he'd probably welcome them in and offer them cake. Anyone stupid enough to think I was cute and cuddly would be easily fooled. But Liz was smart. Liz I thought *maybe* wouldn't be fooled. I was never *entirely* sure, because people like Violet could be pretty clever. But I felt a little bit safe, which was better than nothing.

Also, Liz knew how evil I was, and she didn't get freaked out. Usually, people liked me at first, then they found out how bad I was and dumped me. Liz didn't. She was like a superhero. I could fire evil at her and she just swallowed it up.

Or so I thought.

I liked liking Liz, and being liked, but it was always really, really scary because I knew when she dumped me it would be horrible. Every time she did something cool, I'd think *This won't happen in my new house*, and then I stopped liking it. And she did some really, really cool things. Like finding out where Hayley was, and making her parents let me see her.

My sister Hayley is adopted. Her mummy and daddy were supposed to adopt me too, and I lived with them for nearly a year, but then they changed their mind and sent me back. When they kicked me out, I was supposed to still see Hayley, but I never did. Well, I saw her *once*, but it was weird and awful and Hayley's parents kept glaring at me like I was going to smash Hayley over the head with a chair, which I would never do.

I only did it once to their kid, and it was his fault for being such a moron.

Anyway, I hadn't seen Hayley for three years, but Liz knew all about her, and one Saturday she told me we were going to see her.

I was really nervous. I thought maybe Hayley would have changed, or she'd have forgotten me, or maybe she only liked me because she was little and didn't know any better.

We met Hayley and her dad in a park. She was five the last time I saw her, and now she was eight. She was nearly as tall as me, and her fair hair was darker, and cut short. I said, "I don't like your hair like that, why did you cut it?"

She looked a bit surprised, and said, "I don't know . . . I might be growing it again, I haven't decided." And her dad gave me this look, like, *This is why I didn't want to be your daddy*. I didn't like it, so I grabbed her hand and said, "Let's go play on the swings," and I ran off to the play park, with her running after me to keep up.

When we got to the swings, I said, "You sit on them and I'll push," because that's what we used to do when we were little.

Hayley sat on the swing and I pushed, but it wasn't the same. She was bigger and heavier, and she didn't look like she was enjoying it.

"Why don't you like it?" I said.

"I can push myself now," said Hayley, and she started swinging herself back and forward. I stepped back, feeling stupid and kind of hating her a bit.

"I'm bored of the swings," I said. "Let's play on the climbing frame!" So I ran over to the climbing frame and hauled myself onto the top. Hayley followed, kind of slowly.

There was a row of bars all along the top of the frame. I balanced the soles of my trainers on the bars and raised myself slowly to my feet. Hayley shrieked.

"What are you doing?" She sounded just like she used to when she was little. I started walking along the top of the frame, arms outstretched.

"Olivia!" said Hayley. But at least she looked interested, which she hadn't before. Her dad ran over to us and said, "Olivia, come down this instant!"

I ignored them. I took another step forward, and another, just to prove that I could. Then I dropped on to my knees and swung myself down through the bars. Hayley's dad grabbed my arm and started shaking me.

"What on earth are you doing? Do you want to get yourself killed?"

"That's enough." Liz came forward and put her arm on Hayley's dad's shoulder. "Olivia, I don't think we'll play on the swings any more. Let's go for a walk instead."

I thought about arguing, but I knew if I did, she'd just put me in the car and take me home. So I tugged on Hayley's hand and said, "Come on, let's go."

I thought Hayley would probably hate me now she'd seen Liz and her dad boss me about, and maybe she wouldn't come. But she did.

"Your dad's a moron," I told her. "Do you want me to ask Liz if you can live with us instead?"

Hayley went pink. "I'm OK. . ." she said anxiously. Just for a moment she looked like the Hayley I remembered.

"It's all right," I said. "If you don't want to live with me, I don't care."

"No, it's not. . ." Hayley screwed up her mouth. "I do want to live with you. I do! I just. . . I like my mum and dad too. And they wouldn't let me go anyway."

"I bet they would," I said. "They dumped me. They're going to dump you when you're not cute any more."

Hayley didn't say anything. She looked like she was about to cry. I felt mean. Hayley was the one person who always loved me.

"You're probably OK," I said. "They always liked you better than me. Would you really like to live with me?"

"Of course I would!" said Hayley. I wondered if she meant it. "I cried and cried when you left. Ask my dad if you don't believe me."

I put my arm around her shoulders and gave her a squeeze.

"Sisters for ever," I said. *"For ever."* And she nodded her head up and down, just like I do.

"I *promise*," she said, dead serious.

But I haven't seen her since.

OLD AMELIA

"Who's the woman in the photo?" I asked Jim, that evening. "The really old one, on the landing?"

Jim was in his study, working on his laptop. He didn't look cross at me for interrupting, though.

"Ah. . ." he said. "That's Amelia Dyer. Our celebrity."

"She's famous?" She didn't look famous. She looked too old-fashioned and ugly.

"Well. . ." Jim smiled, "a Victorian celebrity. She was a terribly wicked old lady. She used to live in this house."

"She used to live here? Who was she? What did she do?"

"Slow down," said Jim. "Olivia. Calm down."

"But *who was she*?" I shouted.

"Olivia." Jim looked at me. I wanted to kick him, but I wanted to know about Amelia more. So I just glowered

58

at him, sending bolts of *I hate you* boring into his head and turning his brain to green mush. Jim went on calmly typing. I waited, but he didn't say anything more.

"Who's Amelia Dyer?" I said again. Jim didn't look up. "*Please.*"

Jim beamed at me. "She was a baby farmer," he said. Do you know what a baby farmer is?"

"*No,*" I said. But Jim carried on like he couldn't see my fury.

"Baby farmers were lots of different things," he said. "In Victorian England, if you were a lady who wasn't married, it was very difficult to bring up a child. People wouldn't give you a job, and there weren't enough orphanages for all the babies. So there were all these mothers who had babies, and didn't know what to do with them."

"What happened to them?" I said.

"Well," said Jim, "that's where the baby farmers came in. The best sort of baby farmer was . . . well, sort of like a foster mother – you could leave your baby with her and pay her to look after it while you were at work. Except you'd have to pretend you didn't have a baby, so you couldn't visit it. Some poor women only saw their children every couple of months, and some baby farms were terrible places for a child. Babies lying in cots all day with no one talking to them, or feeding them, or changing their clothes. Lots of babies died in places like that."

I scratched the tabletop with my fingernail. Babies crying and no one looking after them. I hated the way Jim's words made me feel. I said, "Is that what your woman did to her babies?" quickly, so I didn't have to think about it.

"Well, yes," said Jim. "But that wasn't the worst of it. You see, some ladies didn't like the thought of their sons and daughters growing up in places like that. What those ladies wanted was someone nice to adopt their baby and bring it up as their own."

"So why didn't they do that, then?" I asked.

"Well, because there were a lot more babies who needed homes than there were homes for babies. Women had to pay a lot of money to have their child adopted. So women like Amelia Dyer would pretend to be looking for a baby to adopt. They'd take the money and the child and then they'd quietly get rid of it."

"Get rid of it? How? Kill it?"

"That's right. Suffocate it or just let it starve to death."

I went cold. I could just imagine Amelia Dyer. Women on their own are always the worst. I knew it. Amelia Dyer, Violet, my mum. Violet would've killed her foster kids, I bet, if she thought she could get away with it.

"Or sometimes," said Jim, "ladies would come to this house to have their babies. Sometimes Amelia would deliver the baby alive, and sometimes the lady would ask her to deliver it dead. They'd tell the coroner it was a stillbirth and no one would be any the wiser."

"How many babies did she kill?" I whispered.

"Nobody knows," said Jim. "The ladies who used her services didn't exactly shout about it. But she was a baby farmer for most of her life. They think she killed about four hundred children."

"What happened to her?" I asked.

"She was caught," said Jim. "They found the body of a little dead baby floating in the river and they traced it to her. Her trial was very famous. She was found guilty of murder and hanged to death."

"Here?"

"Oh, no. In Reading. She only lived here for a couple of years. She moved around a lot. Much easier to hide when you're moving around."

"But she killed babies here?"

"Well, we don't know for sure," said Jim. "She didn't exactly advertise her murders, either. But, yes, she probably did."

I shivered.

A SENSE OF SMELL

After Jim told me about Amelia Dyer, I decided I didn't care how stupid it looked, I wasn't going to go down the servants' stairs again. But I soon found out that Amelia – or whoever it was – wasn't so easy to avoid.

Smells were the next thing I noticed. There were all these smells in Jim's house which didn't make sense. It took me a while to realize, because in a new house there were *so many* new smells anyway. Mud, and straw, and cat, and chicken poo, and goat, and cut grass, and all the new flowers in the garden – so many different smells all on top of each other, it was a bit overwhelming at first. And then there were the people smells. Jim smelled of Maisy a bit, and coffee, and garlic if he'd been cooking, and farm smells if he'd been feeding the pigs and the goats. Daniel smelled of pencil shavings, and chewing gum, and Zig-Zag. Harriet smelled of strawberry lipgloss, and bubble bath, and the dusty, musty, pencil-y smell from the bottom of the dressing-up box. Grace smelled of Maisy, and foundation, and perfume, and roll-on deodorant.

The first couple of weeks, my nose was too busy learning all this new information, but after a while, I started to notice the other smells. The smells which didn't make any sense.

The fire was one. Jim had a real, actual fire in the living room. It had this thick, woody, ashy smell, which I loved. Mostly, it burned logs. There was a bag of coal too, but nobody used it. One night, though, about a month after I started living there, we ran out of wood and Jim poured some coal on to the fire. The coal smoke definitely smelled different – all metally-enginey-sooty. I didn't like it. Partly because it reminded me of going on steam trains with Grumpy Annabel and Dopey Graham. But partly because I realized that I'd smelled it before in Jim's house when the wood fire was burning.

After that, I often smelled coal smoke. Sometimes I could smell coal, but the fire was only burning wood. Sometimes the fire wasn't even lit. I told Jim, but he didn't seem that surprised.

"It's probably Linda and Dave, or one of the cottages," he said. Linda and Dave lived about five fields away, and the cottages were even further, and over a *hill*. I'd never smelled anything from them before.

There were other smells too. One day, I ran into the

living room after school and smelled tobacco. It really scared me. Cigarettes were part of my mum's smell. I had this memory of her, quick and clear. She used to hold out her arms and say, "Come and have a hug then, pet." And I'd think, *Maybe she likes me after all*, and come running over to be hugged, and she'd stub out her cigarette on my arm and laugh like a madwoman. You'd think after this had happened a couple of times I'd learn, but I never did. Every time she said it, I'd think, *Maybe this time she loves me* and go running back.

I was a stupid kid.

Anyway, so when I smelled cigarettes in Jim's living room, it was like I was five again. I could smell the burnt, roast-meat smell of my arm, and I could hear her laughing. I could even feel my arm starting to burn, and I put my hand on the old scar quickly to stop it hurting. I knew it was just a memory. I knew it wasn't real.

But it *felt* real.

So then Harriet and Daniel came running in after me, and Harriet said, "Do you want to play Batman?" She flung her arms around me, and I jumped about a mile in the air and screamed, "What d'you do that for? Leave me alone!" I pushed her away, hard, so that she fell against the couch with a surprised squeal, and I ran into the kitchen. Jim was unloading the shopping.

"Who's been smoking in the living room?" I said.

Because part of me was worried about my mum. My head knew she probably wasn't there, but my body didn't, and it panicked. And, anyway, it *could* have been her. She could have broken into Social Services and found my file and looked up where I lived. And if it wasn't my mum, that meant it was someone else, someone I didn't know coming into the house without me knowing about it, and maybe being here when I was here, and. . .

"What do you mean?" said Jim, and then Daniel and Harriet were there, and it was all, "Olivia pushed me!" and I couldn't deal with it, so I shoved the shopping off the table, and the bag of tomatoes landed with a wet *thump,* and the apples fell out of their bag and went rolling all over the floor and the bottle of olive oil smashed and oil went everywhere, and I got sent to my room to Think About My Actions Alone. But what I thought was, *Good*, because I got Daniel and Harriet to shut up, and that was even worth having to clean the kitchen up afterwards.

When I came downstairs again, I couldn't smell anything, which was weird. Usually smells stick around for hours and hours. So then I wondered if maybe the smell was in my head, the way the pain in my burnt arm was. I sometimes get memories so strong they come with smells. I tried to ask Jim about it, but he was more interested in talking about me pushing Harriet.

"Olivia," he said, "what just happened? Did you have a flashback?"

But I wouldn't answer.

A flashback was what a jumping-out memory was called. My stupid therapist Helen blahed on about them for ages, but I didn't like thinking about them, so I didn't listen. Something about survival tactics and trauma and blah blah blah blah blah.

After that, I started noticing the tobacco smell more and more. I started worrying that maybe someone was breaking into the house when Jim was away, sitting around smoking fags and watching telly, and then hiding somewhere when he got back. That *really* freaked me out. Jim's house was totally the sort of place you could hide in – there were loads of cupboards and wardrobes and even whole bedrooms that were never used. Someone could have been hiding in my wardrobe or under my bed, waiting to leap out and kidnap me when everyone was asleep. Once I'd thought that, I was even more determined not to let Jim leave me on my own, ever. I wasn't just worried about being forgotten – I was worried about something coming to get me. I didn't know if the person making those smells was someone real, or dead old Amelia haunting me from beyond the grave. Both sounded terrible.

Jim kept trying to send me to my room when I'd done something bad, and I *hated* it. I kept trying to get out of it.

"Olivia, this is important," he said, after I'd come downstairs for about the fourteenth time. "I understand that you get angry sometimes. But you can't throw a screaming fit in the living room when you live with other children. You *have* to find somewhere safe to do it."

And if you don't, I'll chuck you out. The words hung there, unsaid.

*

66

The Saturday after Jim said that, Liz took me to watch Bristol City play. Liz was a massive City fan. So was I. I didn't used to be. I used to say all sorts of rude things about them, just to annoy Liz. It didn't work. But then she took me to a couple of games and I changed my mind. Football matches are brilliant. They're loud and shouty and full of grown-up people swearing at the other team, and calling the players all sorts of rude names. Liz does it too. Normally Liz is very calm, but at football matches she turns into angry, sweary Liz and we have a great time jumping up and down and screaming. Football matches are the only place I've ever been where lots of grown-ups all sing, "You're too fat to referee, you're too fat to refereeeee." It's *fantastic*.

Anyway, after the football we went and got pie and chips and sat in the café talking about the match. Liz said, "What's this about you not going to your room, Olivia? You were so good at that with me."

I was good at that with Liz because I felt safe at Liz's house. If someone had ever tried to kidnap me, she'd have karate-chopped them before they could say "free lollipops".

I said, "I dunno. Can I have a football scarf? All the other kids have one."

Liz didn't even bother to answer me. "Come on, Olivia. You're not stupid. You know how this one is going to end."

I wriggled. Parents shouldn't chuck you out because you won't go to your room. But they do.

"I don't. . ." I said. Then I stopped. Liz waited. "I don't like being on my own," I said. "There are all these *rooms* in Jim's house, and weird smells, and I think there are *people* hiding, and I don't want them to kidnap me. And there's this weird Victorian dead lady, Amelia Dyer, and if it's not people then it's her haunting the house, and I don't want her to catch me on my own. I don't know what she might do to me."

"Olivia," said Liz, "you know there's no such thing as ghosts, right? And you know people can't just walk into Jim's house. He's very careful. He keeps both doors locked all the time."

"But there's *noises*!" I said. "And smells! They can't just come from *nowhere*!"

"OK," said Liz. "So what can we do about it?"

After that, instead of sending me to my room, Jim started sending me to the dining room. The dining room was across the corridor from the kitchen, and it had this door with glass in it, so I could see Jim and Jim could see me, but no one ever used it except at mealtimes, because it was big and cold and didn't have a telly.

I still didn't much like being on my own in the dining room. When I first came to live with the Iveys, I don't think I would have done it. But I could see that Jim was trying. I got why he didn't want me kicking off around Harriet, and I liked that he'd stopped making me go to my room. So even though I didn't like it much, I stayed.

HOME NUMBER 12

ANNABEL AND GRAHAM

Before I moved in with Liz, I lived with Annabel and Graham. They were my second go at a forever family. They came to my foster home and took me to the funfair. Annabel had flat yellow hair and a sort of screwed-in face. Graham had round glasses and a bald spot and a nervous laugh, which he brought out whenever he didn't know what to say.

"Can I go on the dodgems?" I said, the minute we got into the car.

"Course you can," said Graham, giving me a big gooey smile. He let me drive the dodgem, and I bashed it into all the other cars on the floor. It was brilliant.

"Again!" I said, the moment the car stopped moving.

"Don't you want to go on the other rides?" said Graham, but I shook my head as fast as I could.

"I want to go on the dodgems! I've never been to the fair before, and I always wanted to go, and I had a book with pictures in it, and I always thought, if I had a mummy and daddy, they would take me on the dodgems. *Pleeeeeeease!*"

I thought that was going a bit far, and even Dopey Graham would see I was making it up. I'd been to the fair plenty of times with my old mummy and daddy, and even my foster parents had taken me once. But Dopey Graham believed every word.

"Well . . . all right then," he said, grinning like a loon.

We went on the dodgems again, and again, and I could see he wasn't enjoying it quite as much this time.

"How about we go on the merry-go-round?" he said.

"OK. . ." I pulled my saddest face.

"What is it?" he said. "What's the matter?"

"I thought it was my day," I said. I squirmed like I was really shy. "To do whatever I wanted."

"Sweetheart, of course it is!" said Graham. He looked horrified.

"Good," I said. "I want to go on the dodgems!"

In the end, we went on the dodgems eleven times in a row. I only let him stop when he promised to buy me a candyfloss *and* a bag of popcorn *and* a packet of crisps. I totally ignored Grumpy Annabel. She looked right peeved off.

"I love you, Daddy!" I told Dopey Graham, and he gave me this goofy grin and bought me a chocolate éclair.

I was sick in the car on the way home, but I didn't

70

care. I made sure I threw up all over Grumpy Annabel. I knew this family wasn't going to be any trouble.

I was going to be boss.

I was boss right from the first day I moved in. I was pretty small – I was only seven, and I was the littlest in my class – and I could tell Dopey Graham thought I was sweet.

"Isn't she adorable?" he used to say. I'd run to the door as he came home from work, and give him my biggest hug.

"I love you, Daddy!" I'd say, and he'd give me a Kinder Egg, or a bag of sweets, or a comic.

I never had so much to eat as I did when I lived with Graham and Annabel. My old foster mother, Lynne, told them I had problems with food.

"It's a fairly common side-effect of early neglect," she said, when she thought I wasn't listening. "You just need to make sure she has clear boundaries."

"Poor little thing," said Graham. "No wonder she's worried about food if she didn't have enough to eat. Surely when she finds out we're going to feed her, she'll be fine."

Ha.

The first few weeks I lived with them, they used to let me eat whatever I wanted. I would take food and hide it under my bed, so I wouldn't go hungry. They told me it was my house now, and I could help myself. The first night I was there, I didn't eat anything Grumpy Annabel cooked, but after they'd gone to bed I ate six packets of crisps, a whole packet of chocolate biscuits, five mini pork pies, three leftover sausages and most of a jar of chocolate spread. Then I went upstairs and was sick in Grumpy Annabel's knicker drawer. She went bright pink when she found out, so I started to cry and said my tummy hurt.

"Poor baby! Of course it does!" said Dopey Graham.

"I want to go home!" I said.

"Of course you do," said Dopey Graham. He lifted me on to his knee. I took the chance to be sick again on his pyjamas.

After that, Grumpy Annabel said I couldn't just take food any time I wanted.

"But you promised!" I wailed. "You promised, and now you've lied to me just like everybody else!"

"Oh, baby," said Dopey Graham. He gave me a hug, and I put my arms around his neck and squeezed him so tight he nearly choked. "Of course you can go into the kitchen. We just don't want you to make yourself poorly again."

"But—" said Grumpy Annabel. I could tell she hadn't forgotten her sicky knickers. "We can't just let her eat whatever she wants!"

"She won't," said Dopey Graham. "Will you, baby?"

I hiccuped, and glanced at Grumpy Annabel triumphantly.

"No, Daddy," I said.

But I did.

Grumpy Annabel stopped buying sweets, in the hope that that would stop me. It didn't. The day she stopped getting sweets, I ate twelve jam sandwiches, and none of the roast chicken she'd spent all morning cooking.

Grumpy Annabel and Dopey Graham had a huge fight about it.

"This is *pathological*," Annabel said. "She's doing it to get at me."

"Oh, love," said Graham. "She's only little! You're making her sound like a criminal mastermind. What sort of child makes herself ill just to get at her parents?"

"This one does," said Grumpy Annabel. "You don't know her like I do. She's all sweetness and light around you. She hates me."

"She doesn't hate you," said Dopey Graham. There was a pause, while I guessed he must be snuggling her. They were like big teddy bears – they snuggled all the time. "I know it's hard," he said. "I know you're tired. But she'll get over this, when she realizes she's not going to starve."

"I wonder if Lynne might have been right. . ." said Annabel.

"Lynne also said we have to let her see she can trust us," said Graham. "I don't want to break a promise to a child. Especially not this one."

But even Dopey Graham realized he had to do something. Their solution was Olivia's Special Food Box. Annabel would fill it with Healthy Food like muesli bars and bread sticks, and if I was hungry, I was supposed to eat something from there.

"And if I eat your food. . .?" I said.

"Then you have to have a time out," said Grumpy Annabel.

Time outs were how you got punished in the Dopey house. If you were bad, you had to sit on the sofa for seven minutes and not talk. It was a stupid idea though, because Annabel could never make me do it.

The first afternoon I wasn't supposed to steal from the kitchen, I took one of Grumpy Annabel's chocolate muffins from the fridge. I picked a muffin, because she'd bought three of them, so it was really obvious when one of them was gone. I left the wrapper out on the table just to make sure.

I was upstairs drawing pictures on Annabel's bedroom wall when she found out. I could hear her feet going into the kitchen. Then there was this long pause. I could hear her being frightened, which made me giggle. I loved that Grumpy Annabel was about five times as old as me, and I made her frightened.

She came upstairs, saw me drawing on her wall, and took a deep breath.

"Olivia, did you eat this?" she said, holding out the muffin wrapper.

I shook my head. "Uh-uh."

I drew a muffin on the wall.

"Olivia! Stop that!" She grabbed the marker pen from my hand. I squealed.

"I was playing with that!"

"Olivia, listen to me! Did you eat the muffin?"

What sort of idiot was she? Of course I ate the muffin. Who else could have done?

"Daddy did it."

"Daddy's at work," said Annabel. She grabbed my arm. "You need a time out. Seven minutes for the muffin, and seven minutes for lying to me."

And nothing for drawing on the wall? Cool. But she still needed to learn that she couldn't boss me.

"I *won't*!" I said. And I spat in her face.

Grumpy Annabel's eyes narrowed. She picked me up. I shrieked and started kicking.

"You're hurting! You're hurting!"

Grumpy Annabel started dragging me out of the room. I grabbed on to the door frame with both hands.

"I *hate* you!"

She reached out a hand to peel my fists away, leaving one arm around my waist. I lunged forward and bit through her sleeve, hard enough to draw blood. She let go. I ran back into her bedroom and slammed the door. Annabel started pushing against it and I pushed back, feet jammed against the chest of drawers.

"You can't make me!" I yelled. I knew that would make her angry, and it did. She shoved the door, hard. I laughed at her.

"You're bigger than me, and you still can't make me do anything!"

Grumpy Annabel pushed the door hard enough to get inside. I scrambled to my feet and ran over to the dressing-table. I started picking up her ornaments and throwing them on to the floor, where they smashed into a million pieces. She always got mad when I broke her things.

"*I'm* the boss! *I'm* the boss!" I yelled.

"Olivia!" said Grumpy Annabel. "Olivia, please. Stop it!" She was nearly crying. "Olivia, that belonged to my granny. Please—"

I lifted the ornament – a stupid lady in a big skirt – over my head. I looked her straight in the eye and I laughed at her. Then I threw the lady down on to their stupid wooden floor.

SMASH.

Grumpy Annabel lost it. She grabbed my arm and dragged me into my room.

"You want to know what it's like when someone breaks something you love?" she said. "You want to know what that feels like?" She snatched the doll that my mum gave me, the last time I saw her. I shrieked, but she held it high over her head. "You see this doll?" she said. "This doll is going in the bin. I mean it, Olivia. You can't treat other people's things like that."

I spat in her eye.

"You won't take my dolly from me," I said. "Stupid bitch."

And I started pulling the things that they'd bought me from the cupboard – the board games, and the cuddly toys, and the Barbie dolls – and tearing them to bits.

I was still in my room when Dopey Graham came home. I heard him say, "*What?*" and Annabel crying.

"But what about time outs?" he said.

After a while, I heard his footsteps clumping upstairs. I climbed into bed and pulled the duvet over my head. He came into the room and sat down beside me.

"You've been being naughty, princess," he said. I pulled the duvet down.

"Mummy took my dolly," I said. "The one my real mum gave me. She said I couldn't have it any more."

"I know, sweetheart," said Dopey Graham. "But you were very naughty, weren't you? You shouldn't have broken Mummy's lady."

I looked away. "I was scared," I said. "I thought she was going to hit me, like my mummy used to."

"Oh, baby," said Dopey Graham. He put his arm around me. "No one's going to hit you in this house."

"Mummy took my dolly," I whispered.

"I know, princess," said Graham. "But you have to do what Mummy tells you. What did she want you to do?"

"Have a time out."

"Come on, then," said Dopey Graham. He led me downstairs and sat me on the sofa. "Seven minutes," he said, and he kissed me on the top of my head.

I sat perfectly still with my toes pointed downwards and my hands neatly folded in my lap. I pulled my skirt out so the ballerina ruffles flowed down around me. I looked like a little girl ornament from Grumpy Annabel's dressing-table.

"Well done, princess!" said Dopey Graham, after six and a half minutes exactly. "Now come and say sorry to Mummy."

Grumpy Annabel was sitting in the kitchen with tearmarks on her face and a big glass of wine. *I did that*, I thought.

"What do you say?" said Dopey Graham.

"Sorry, Mummy," I whispered.

"Good girl," said Dopey Graham. He reached under the table and brought out my dolly. "There you go! No one's *ever* going to take her away again. I promise."

I wrapped my arms around the doll and buried my face in her hair. She smelled of old tea bags and rotten vegetables. She smelled of the rubbish bin.

"Thank you, Daddy," I said, and I shot Grumpy Annabel a triumphant look. Who's the boss now?

ZOMBIE KILLING SPREES

I liked Harriet. It took me a while to realize why I liked her so much. I think it was because she reminded me of living with my sister Hayley. Harriet was eight, which was nearly as old as Hayley. Hayley was nine. That was the only thing similar about them, though. Hayley had yellow hair and blue eyes, and she didn't like it when I didn't do what I was told, which was always. She liked Polly Pocket and she had a pink T-shirt and jeans with a heart on the pocket. Actually, I didn't know very much about Hayley. I'd only seen her twice since she was five. When she was five, I was her favourite person in the world, but she probably liked her mum and dad better now.

Harriet liked me, though. Harriet was great. She was little and dark-haired, and she was way easy to wind up, because she took everything dead seriously. Her best thing was pretending and dress-up. She had a whole box of dress-up toys, and as soon as she came home from school she would run and put on some fairy wings, or a crown, or a pirate costume. She never cared how stupid she looked.

After pretending, Harriet liked drawing best. She looked all little and sweet, but she wasn't. She liked really gruesome stories about ghosts and flesh-eating insects and zombies. The more blood, the better. Her pictures were the same. She'd draw puppies and kittens and bunnies with eyeballs falling out and blood dripping down their cheeks.

"Well, I suppose it's creative," said Jim, when Harriet presented him with one of her pictures. "But don't show it to Social Services, will you?"

I think Jim was a bit worried when I came about whether I'd beat Harriet up, but I never did. I liked Harriet. I liked playing little-kid games. I liked playing with the dolls' house, pulling all the furniture out and arranging it exactly right in all the rooms. Harriet's dolls' house was big and square. Her dad had made it for her. Sometimes I liked to put everything in perfectly, and sometimes I liked to turn it all upside down, chuck the parents' bed out into the garden, fill their room with all the kids' toys and put the mum in the toilet.

I played with Harriet quite a lot. She always let me be boss. It was like having a small, wriggly slave in fairy wings. I played with Daniel too, but if Daniel disagreed with me he wouldn't shut up about it, and he never did what he was told like Harriet did.

Being bigger than Harriet meant it was my job to look after her. Normally it was other people's job to look after me, and normally they were rubbish at it. I was great at looking after Harriet. I don't think she was always very happy. She was happy at home, but I don't think she liked school very much. She had these two best friends, who were sort of best friends with each other really and let her tag along when it suited them, and then told her to get lost when it didn't. Whenever they had to pick partners or someone to sit next to, they picked each other, and they had all these secrets and jokes they didn't let Harriet in on.

"Why d'you hang around with those losers?" I said, and she looked sort of unhappy and mumbled, *They're my friends*. Huh.

One day, when I'd been living with Jim for about two months, I was playing football at lunchtime, and I saw Harriet and these two girls. They had one of Harriet's shoes, and they were playing Piggy-in-the-middle with it, chucking it to each other while Harriet ran between them going, "That's mine! Give it back!"

The girls were laughing like it was a game, but Harriet was almost crying. The tarmac was all cold and wet and covered in mud. Piggy-in-the-middle is a pretty rubbish game for piggy, and Harriet was hopping about on one foot, trying not to get her sock wet, so you could see she was probably never going to get the shoe back anyway.

No one else seemed to care. Not the teachers, not anyone. I marched over to the biggest kid, and yanked the shoe out of her hands.

"That's Harriet's!" I said. "Why didn't you give it back when she asked you to?"

"It's only a game!" the kid said, all innocent. "We're just having some fun!"

"It wasn't fun for *Harriet*," I said. I gave Harriet her shoe. "She's supposed to be your friend!"

The girl looked kind of embarrassed and defensive at the same time. If someone had told me off like that, I'd have told them to butt out, but this kid was only about eight.

"It's only a game. . ." she said again, but she sounded a bit doubtful.

"You were being horrible," I told her. "Be nice to Harriet. Or else!"

After that, I used to keep an eye out for Harriet at school. If the other girls were being mean to her, I'd go over and make sure they stopped. Sometimes Harriet would run and find me at breaktime.

"Olivia! Come and play!" she'd say, and sometimes I would and sometimes I wouldn't. It all depended how I felt.

It was Harriet who told me about Amelia Dyer's ghost. I still didn't like the picture of Amelia on the staircase. I thought about breaking her, or hiding her, but the wall looked even creepier when I took the picture down. Like she was still there somehow, only now I didn't know where she was. I worried she was maybe wandering around the house, like that time I heard footsteps on the stairs with no one in them, and maybe that was her, haunting me. I put it back, quick.

"She's one creepy lady," I told Daniel and Harriet.

"She haunts the house," said Harriet. "She *kills* people."

"She doesn't *kill* people," said Daniel uneasily. "Not . . . exactly."

"How could a ghost kill someone?" I said. "Ghosts just walk through stuff. They couldn't even pick a knife up."

"Stupid! She doesn't *kill* people," said Harriet. "She scares them so hard they just *die*. And then she *possesses* them and makes them do what she wants. They go on *rampages*."

Harriet said "rampages" in the same voice other little kids use to say "ice cream" or "Disneyland". Violet used to go on rampages. She never killed anyone, at least not while I lived with her, but it wasn't much like Disneyland.

"How can she possess you after you're dead?" I said. "Does she turn people into zombies? Wouldn't people have noticed?"

"Don't count on it," said Grace, from the sofa, where she was curled up feeding Maisy.

Daniel sighed. "There weren't any zombies, and there weren't any rampages," he said. "It's just . . . this is an unlucky house, that's all. There are lots of stories about Amelia Dyer haunting it. People say you can hear babies crying, and there's this kid as well – a little girl she's supposed to have killed. People heard her running down the corridors. And there's one woman who used to live here, who killed herself. And before she died she kept saying Amelia Dyer was talking to her, telling her to kill her husband and her little boy. She turned on the gas in the oven and tried to poison everyone in the house, but her husband woke up and turned it off, so she was the only one who died. Dad says she wasn't possessed, though. She was just sad. Or mad. Or both."

"You don't know that," said Harriet. "Amelia could have possessed her! Anyway, it's not just her, there's another story too."

"Yes. . ." said Daniel. "But the other story is even more stupid. There's supposed to be this girl who lived here years and years ago. She was a servant, and she was in love with one of the boys who worked on the farm, and he got her pregnant. She asked him to marry her, but he wouldn't, so she had the baby, and then she had to leave her job. She didn't have anywhere to live, so she had to sleep under hedges, and the baby was cold and sick and she couldn't look after it. So she strangled the baby and left it on the doorstep with a note, to shame the boy. But Amelia didn't kill her. She got hanged for baby murder. It wasn't anything to do with being possessed. People just say that because it's a good story."

"Well, she *might* have been possessed," said Harriet. "And, anyway, that's three murderers in one house – how many houses have *three* murderers in them?"

"It's an old house," said Daniel. "And the suicide lady wasn't a murderer, 'cause her husband stopped her. And we don't even know the other story's true. It's just something the guy who runs the pub told us. He also said the pub's haunted by a mad highwayman who shoots you if you go to the loo without buying a drink. I think he just made it up."

"I bet he didn't," said Harriet. "I bet it's true!"

"It *isn't* true," I said. "Ghosts aren't real. They *aren't*!"

But after Harriet and Daniel told me about Amelia's ghost, I started to notice even more creepy things which didn't make any sense. I am a very noticing sort of person. I'd been living in Jim's house for less than a month, but I could always tell when Grace was in a bad mood or just an at-a-good-bit-in-my-book mood from the way her shoulders hunched. I could always tell whether Zig-Zag was really asleep or just pretending. Noticing things is another one of my superpowers. It's very useful when you're trying to wind someone up to know whether they care more about how fat they are, or how good a mother, or how late they're going to be for work, or whatever.

"You don't have to watch us all the time, Olivia," Dopey Graham used to say. "You're safe here! Nobody's going to hurt you." But then he dumped me with Liz and never even came to visit, so that shows how much I could trust *him*. I always watched everyone, always. I never felt completely safe, ever.

That next month, I heard three babies crying who *definitely* weren't Maisy. The first time, Maisy was asleep. The second, she and Grace weren't even *in the house*. And the third time, Harriet and I were *in the same room* as her, building a tower out of bricks for her to knock over. She was laughing, and another baby was crying, somewhere in the house. I made Harriet stop and listen, but she couldn't hear anything. I wasn't that surprised. Even with supersonic hearing I had to strain to catch it.

It wasn't just babies either. I was in my room one evening, amusing myself by drawing rude pictures of Jim on my walls, when I heard this noise. It sounded like someone running down the corridor outside. Someone small, like a kid, but I could tell just from the sound of the feet that it wasn't Daniel or Harriet. I was so surprised that I stopped drawing and waited. After about for ever, the footsteps came back. They ran past my door and then stopped. They didn't go down the stairs, or into one of the rooms. They just stopped.

I opened my door and looked out. No one was there. I looked left, then right, and then I heard them again: footsteps, running right past me with no feet in them, no person running, no one there at all.

A real, proper ghost. Definitely.

I wasn't afraid. I don't know why, I ought to have been. Mostly I was curious. I stood there in the doorway for ages, waiting, but whatever it was didn't come back. So I shut the door and went back inside, to draw black footprints all around the windowpanes.

THE PAST (COMING TO GET ME)

My brother Jamie was six when I moved in with the Iveys, but I hadn't seen him since he was a baby. He was adopted almost immediately, and I didn't suppose I'd ever see him again. When we first went into care, I used to ask about him all the time, but now I'd sort of got used to not having him around. I still thought about him, though.

Living with a baby again was weird. Mostly, I liked Maisy. I liked how happy she was. I liked how you just had to say, "Hey, Maisy-face!" or play Peepo! or something with her and she'd start giggling like crazy. I liked how when I came into the room she'd lift up her arms, and you'd know that if she could talk, she'd be saying "Up!" I'd pick her up and carry her around. She'd look happy for about two seconds and then she'd hold out her arms to Daniel, as if to say, *I am the Queen of the Universe and you are all my slaves*. I liked that. I liked that she was so sure people would do what she told them to, and I liked that, actually, people usually did.

What I didn't like was the way she made me feel when she cried. She didn't cry loads, but when she did she really went at it. She'd screw up her face and howl and howl and howl. I hated it right from the start. It made me feel small and scared and full of worry. Like something bad was going to happen and I didn't know what.

Maisy crying wasn't something I could do much about. At first, I used to shout, "Stop it! Stop it!" but that just made her cry louder and Grace would start swearing at me. Then I used to run out of the room with my hands over my ears, but that meant I was on my own, which made things *worse*. When you're small and scared and full of worry, you want to be with people.

Jim tried talking to me.

"She's only a baby, Olivia. She's happy again now – why don't we go in and see?"

And, most of the time, he was right. Maisy went from "The worst thing ever in the universe just happened to me and everything is over!" to "Oh, look, a crayon," in about five seconds. But I'd still be freaked out.

One afternoon, Daniel and I were watching *X-Men* in the living room. Grace was playing with Maisy, building a house out of her A Level files, while Maisy pulled it down. Grace had balanced Psychology on top of Economics and History. Maisy tugged at History and the whole thing came crashing down on top of her. She fell backwards and started howling.

"Make her shut up!" I yelled. Grace picked up Maisy and started joggling her up and down, but Maisy screwed up her face and wouldn't stop.

"Make him stop that right now!" someone yells in my head. *It's my mum. Jamie's crying, and I can't make him stop. I'm going to get in trouble. I hold him like Grace holds Maisy, but he's heavy, because I'm only five, and little. Why does he have to keep screaming like that? Doesn't he know it's me my mum will be angry with?*

I could feel the weight of Jamie in my arms. I could smell wet baby, and spilled cider, and my mum's cigarettes. I knew I was in Jim's living room, but for a moment it was like five-year-old Olivia had come to live in eleven-year-old Olivia's body, and because she was angrier and more afraid than me, she sort of took over. I wanted to cry and I wanted to hit something, and I wanted someone – Liz – to hold me and tell me I was safe.

Jamie – no, Maisy – was still howling. Daniel was watching *X-Men* like nothing had happened. I sat there on the floor with my arms round my legs, struggling to come back to myself, and then it happened. I felt a sudden rush of hatred and evil. It felt like something had smacked me in the face, except instead of actually smacking me, it had slammed all this concentrated hatred straight at me.

I knew who it was, of course. It was her. Amelia Dyer. Amelia Dyer, telling me how much she hated me.

I hunched myself into as small a ball as I could, and buried my face into my knees, and wished and wished and wished that she'd go away.

Wishes are for losers. They never come true.

HOME NUMBER 11

LYNNE AND JOHN

Before I lived with Graham and Annabel, I was with these foster parents called Lynne and John. Social Services moved me there after they finally noticed what my old foster mother Violet was doing to her foster kids. They were looking for someone to adopt me, but I knew they wouldn't find anyone.

I didn't do very well with Lynne and John. I was pretty frightened after what had happened with Violet. I had nightmares. I wet the bed. All the things that happened with Violet got muddled in my head with the things that had happened with my mum. I started remembering scary things that had happened at my mum's house and I'd forgotten till now – like the time she held my hand against the electric hob until my skin cooked, or the time she made me eat rotten meat as a punishment for stealing food. I was very bad at Lynne and John's house, because I was very scared. I was scared they wouldn't give me enough to eat, and I was scared they'd hurt me when I was bad. I shouted all sorts of awful things at Lynne, and when they made me go to school, I did all I could to get sent home. When I got home, I used to run straight upstairs and hide in bed. John gave me this old radio that I used to take under the blankets with me so I could listen to the music on loud and try and forget about Mum, and Violet, and everything else in the world.

Lynne and John were nice enough, I suppose. They didn't make me do chores, and they didn't care if I didn't do my homework, and they didn't get angry when I got scared. I'd be in a shopping centre or at the supermarket, somewhere normal, and all of a sudden I'd start to panic. I'd start breathing really fast, like I was drowning in air, and I'd think I was going to die. I'd get all filled up with fright, and I'd start to cry, and want to run away as fast as I could. John was very nice when that happened. He'd kneel down beside me and talk to me, saying, "It's OK, Olivia. I'm here. You're safe. It's OK."

Lynne and John didn't like me though. No one ever likes me. I heard Lynne talking on the phone about me.

"There's nothing unexpected. It's just . . . exhausting. She's such a needy kid. And some of the things she comes out with! Honestly, I could throttle that child's mother. Some people ought to be sterilized." She was quiet while the person on the other end of the phone said something. "No, I know. I just . . . she watches me all the time, like

I'm about to start doing God knows what to her. Home should be somewhere safe, you know? Not somewhere where you have to hear about all the terrible things people do to children."

I didn't know what sterilized meant then, but I do now. It's something you do to people to stop them having children. What she meant was that my mum was evil, and she ought to have been sterilized, so she couldn't have kids who were evil like me.

I didn't like living there after I heard that, but I wasn't happy when Lynne told me I was going to be adopted. I wanted a family, but I knew that this new one wouldn't keep me, so I didn't see the point of moving in with them, just to have it all fall to pieces again.

EACH LITTLE BIRD THAT SINGS

Daniel and Harriet had lots of family. Not just Jim and their mum (who lived in Brazil, and called them every fortnight and sent them funny postcards and Brazilian sweets, but never sent me anything, ever, which Jim said was fair enough because she'd never met me, but I thought was totally unfair. I thought Jim ought to have bought me presents to even things out, but he never did). They *also* had grannies and grandads and aunties and uncles and first, second, third, fourth and fifth cousins once, twice and forty-seven times removed.

I don't even have grandparents. Or if I do I've never seen them. They never came to visit me once all the time I was in foster care. I have a mum (but I don't know where she is) and Hayley (who I never get to see because her mum and dad hate me) and Jamie (but I don't know where he lives or if he's still called Jamie or *anything*).

Maybe somewhere I've got family; aunts and uncles and grandparents and maybe even a dad. I had a dad once, but my mum says he was a useless lump. Maybe he wasn't so bad, though. If he met me, maybe he'd love me, the way other people's dads love them. Maybe all my family would love me. Maybe they've just been busy for the last five years – being abroad or something, and no one told them about us – and maybe one day they'll call up Social Services and adopt me and I'll have a real family, like Daniel and Harriet.

Or maybe not.

Anyway, this Saturday I wasn't going to see Liz, because I was going to Daniel and Harriet's Auntie Abigail's wedding. Harriet was a bridesmaid in a pink dress with lots of lace, but I wasn't even a ring-bearer. I didn't want to go *at all*. I knew it would be dreadful. I moaned and wailed and whined and whinged, but Jim wouldn't listen.

"You're part of our family now, Olivia," he said.

"If I'm part of your family then how come *I'm* not a bridesmaid?" I said.

"Well. Yes. That's because this madness has been in production for nearly two years, the bridesmaids' dresses have been finished for half a year, and you've been a part of our family for three months."

"You could buy me a dress," I said. "It's not hard, buying dresses. It takes an afternoon!"

"I'm sorry, Olivia," said Jim. "If I was getting married,

you could be *my* bridesmaid."

Huh. It was totally unfair. Particularly because Grace didn't even have to go. She and Maisy were going to some stupid university open day in London.

"What if *I* wanted to go to a university open day?" I said.

"If you've been given a conditional offer from the London School of Economics and forgotten to tell me about it, then, yes," said Jim. "Otherwise no."

Harriet was all squeaky about being a bridesmaid. For the whole week before the wedding she kept blabbing on about hair slides, and make-up, and wedding rehearsals, and jewellery, and all sorts of stupid stuff. It made me want to cut her bridesmaid's dress into tiny little pieces and set them on fire. I would have done too, but the dress was at Auntie Abigail's house.

"Who cares about being a stupid bridesmaid?" I told Harriet. "You're just going to look fat and ugly in a stupid pink dress. Bridesmaids always look like losers, they're supposed to, to make the bride look better."

Harriet's lip started quivering. She glanced at me, and then at Daniel. Daniel sighed.

"That's a bit harsh, Olivia," he said.

"It is *not* harsh! It's the *truth*! She—"

"All right." Jim appeared out of nowhere and grabbed my arm. "Come here, Olivia."

And then I had to sit through *yet another* long talk about jealousy, and Harriet, and being nice, and then help Jim chop up gazillions of carrots for dinner.

I was in a horrible mood on the day of the wedding. Auntie Abigail and Uncle David were adventure capitalists in London. I wasn't exactly sure what adventure capitalists did. Probably they went on adventures and captured pirate ships and dug up buried treasure from Amazonian rainforests. It was definitely something like that, because they were both stinking rich. The wedding was going to be well posh. Daniel had a grown-up-looking green shirt. Jim had a suit. I had a red dress which Grumpy Annabel had bought me, and which looked like it had been made for a seven-year-old (it had). It only still fitted because I'm so little. I'm smaller than Harriet, and she's nearly three years younger than I am. I don't care. I get loads of good stuff from looking little.

The first thing I did when I got into the car was spill Coke accidentally-on-purpose down my dress. I screamed at Jim to take me back home and let me put something else on, but he just kept driving. I screamed and screamed, but he wouldn't stop.

We dropped Harriet off at her granny's house to have her hair done with Auntie Abigail and the other bridesmaids. Daniel and Harriet's granny came out to the car to see us.

"How lovely! You're here! Do you want to come and have a cup of tea?"

"Not a good idea," said Jim, glancing at me. I put on my best talking-to-strangers face.

"*I'd* like a cup of tea. I'm *so* excited about the wedding.

97

Can I come and see the bridesmaids' dresses? *Please*, Granny."

"I don't see why not—" Granny began, but Jim shook his head.

"I'm a cruel and unusual father," he said. "And the answer's no. Give me a kiss, Harriet, pet, and we'll see you at the church."

The wedding didn't start until two, so Jim took Daniel and me to the park. We played cricket, and football, and we took our skateboards on the skateboard ramps and Jim let us play on them for ages, even in our fancy wedding clothes. I got mud streaks all the way up my legs to go with my Coke stains, but Jim didn't care. I would have stayed in the park all day, but finally he said we had to go and have lunch. I may have kicked and fought a bit then, but only because I was having such a good time, just me and Daniel and Jim.

We had sausage and chips at the park café. And then it was time for the wedding.

Daniel had been to lots of weddings, and he told me they were always hideous.

"Weddings are just grown-ups droning on and people reading naff poetry about love," he said. "And photographs. And you have to tell the bride she looks pretty even if she looks like a whale with lacy bits."

"Can't Daniel and I play on our skateboards out here?" I said. Daniel looked hopeful, but Jim was firm.

"In! And if you want any cake – behave!"

The wedding was even more boring than I'd thought

it would be. We had to sit for ages waiting. Then Auntie Abigail came down the aisle and everyone went, *Oooh*. I don't know why. Auntie Abigail was fat and ugly, and her wedding dress was too small, so there was this roll of fat spilling out of her top. Harriet's bridesmaid dress was pink and frothy and stupid.

Someone read a poem, and then they started singing a hymn. I kicked along to it on the back of the pew in front of us. This old man turned round and gave me an evil look. I stuck my tongue out, and he looked horrified. Ha!

Daniel looked as bored as I did.

I nudged him. "Want to play thumb war?"

Daniel glanced at Jim, who was wearing his I'm-going-to-pretend-I-can't-see-you-and-hope-you-go-away face.

"Sure," he said.

We played four games of thumb war, which started out quiet-ish, and ended with Daniel twisting my arm so hard that I fell off my seat and knocked the hymn books off the shelf and on to the floor. Several people in big hats turned round and said, "*Shhh!*" very loudly.

"You *shhh!*" I said indignantly. "Your *shhh*ing is just as loud as Daniel and me! How can people hear what's going on when you're all going *shhh*?"

"OK, OK," said Jim. He put his hand on my arm. "Calm down, Olivia."

Huh. I crossed my arms and slid down my seat until my bum was nearly hanging off the edge. Daniel saw what I was doing and copied me. I slid out further. So did Daniel. Now I was only clinging on with my elbows.

Daniel pushed himself out even further and landed on the floor with a *thump*.

"Kids!" said Jim. "Behave!"

"It was Daniel!" I squealed.

"Can we all rise—" said the bloke in the dress at the front of the church. All around us people were getting to their feet and fumbling in their hymn books.

"It's a song!" I said. "We like songs, don't we, Daniel? What song is it?"

It was "The Battle Hymn of the Republic". Daniel looked at me and I looked at him. We both giggled.

I knew "The Battle Hymn of the Republic". Daniel knew it too because we sang it at school, and the boys had a silly version they sang in the playground. I could see Daniel was thinking the same thing as me, because as the organ starting *boop*ing and the people started singing, we both opened our mouths and sang:

"Mine eyes have seen the glory,
Of the burning of the school.
We have tortured every teacher,
We have broken every rule.
We have marched down to the headmaster,
To tell him he's a fool.
The school is burning do-o-own."

People turned round to look. Jim grabbed our elbows and marched us out into the porch.

"What did I tell you?" he said.

"What did *I* tell *you*?" I said. "You should have let us stay out here and play skateboards!"

"You are going to sit there," said Jim, pointing to a bench. "And you are going to *behave*."

We sat down. We both of us still wanted to giggle. Jim sat on the bench opposite. He gave us a stern look. We sat in silence for a whole almost-ten-seconds. Then Daniel started to hum. I joined in. Jim looked away. He was trying not to laugh. Inside the church, the wedding people were all still singing. We opened our mouths and we all sang together:

"Glory, glory, hallelujah.
Teacher hit me with a ruler.
So I hit her in the belly,
And she wobbled like a jelly,
And she ain't gonna teach no more no mo-o-ore."

I loved it. Me and Daniel and Jim, all being silly together.

CLOSE YOUR PRETTY EYES

But back at Jim's house, there was Amelia Dyer. Worst of all, there was Amelia at night.

I've never liked the night. Night is when you're in the most danger, because you're on your own and everyone else is asleep. I *hate* sleep. If I was God, people would never sleep. *Anything* could happen to you. Bad people could come into your room and steal your stuff, like the big girls in Fairfields used to, or good people could walk out on you (my mum used to do this to us), and you wouldn't even *know* until the morning.

Except I would. I'd wake up. I *always* wake up. I don't think I've ever gone to sleep and then not woken up until morning. Even in Liz's house, I never did.

Amelia didn't start coming for me in the night until I'd been living with Jim for a while. I'm not sure why. Maybe she was scoping me out, trying to work out what sort of person I was. She didn't come after anyone else. At first, I thought it was just because I noticed things that other people didn't, because they didn't have super noticing senses like I did. But when she *really* started coming after me, I knew it couldn't be that, because you'd have to be deaf, blind and *dead* not to notice her. So then I thought maybe it was something about *me*. Like maybe she had some demonic purpose and I was the person she needed to make whatever it was happen. Although if she *did* have a demonic purpose, you'd think she'd just tell me what it was, instead of making me hear footsteps and smell mysterious smells, and looming over me all evil. A message in blood on my wall saying KILL EVERYONE would have made a lot more sense.

The night Amelia really started coming after me, I woke up, as usual, and the first thing I did was listen. Were there noises? Was anyone there? Was I safe?

So I lay there listening, and I heard this noise. It was another baby noise, but this time the baby wasn't crying. It was just making wet, gurgly noises, the sort babies *do* make, when they're left on their own. It didn't exactly sound unhappy. It was just sort of talking away to itself.

It was in my room.

I sat up, listening, all tense and waiting, and I heard it again. A sort of *Ah!* baby noise. I was terrified. I couldn't see much, but I could see enough to know that the door was shut and there was no baby there on the floor.

I crawled back up the bed, as far away from the baby noises as I could get. I wanted to run and find Jim, or Daniel, or anyone warm and alive. But leaving would have meant going past whatever it was that was making the baby noises, and I didn't want to get any nearer. I would have shouted, but my mouth had stopped working. I tried to say, "Help" and all that came out was, "Heh—" Not even someone with supersonic hearing would have heard that.

I sat there for what felt like ages, just listening. I was really frightened. I felt like I was going to die. I started doing what I used to do when I lived with Violet, which was chant things to myself in my head, over and over and over, until I could forget that Violet was spraying me with cold water, or making me stand on one leg in the corner, or whatever. *Mary, Mary, quite contrary, how does your garden grow? With silver bells, and cockle shells, and pretty maids all in a row. Mary, Mary, quite contrary, how does your garden grow?. . .* It was a pretty stupid song, but it meant I could concentrate on chanting and didn't have to think about the baby in my room. And *what might happen next.*

Then the door opened.

It *creaked* open dead slowly. I stared at it in horror. I knew it wasn't Jim on the other side, I *knew* it. I'd have heard him coming, and I hadn't. I hadn't heard *anyone* coming.

This is a song that never ends. It goes on and on, my friends. Some people started singing it, not knowing what it was. And now they're always singing it for ever just because. . . This is a song that never ends. . .

The door opened. *Something* was there, something holding a big old-fashioned smuggler's lantern, but the hand which held the lantern wasn't there, the body which held the hand was gone, there was just the lantern hanging in the darkness with no one to carry it. The someone crossed the room on big heavy feet which made the floorboards creak. She was coming towards me. She was going to. . .

The footsteps stopped, about an arm's length away from the bed. There was another creak as the invisible person picked up the baby. The baby made a gurgly gasp. Then, horribly, the invisible person began to sing.

"Go to sleep, my baby, close your pretty eyes." It was a lady's voice, an old, raspy, tobacco-ruined voice. It was old Amelia, I knew it was. *"Angels up above you are peeking through the skies."* It terrified me, that voice. I could feel the hatred practically burning off the lady, just like I used to feel it from my mother when I was little. She hated that baby. I always know when people are dangerous, and Amelia was dangerous all right. She was big and old and mean and full of anger. She was looking for something to hurt, and that little baby was it. *"Great big moon is shining, stars begin to peep. It's time for little babies to go to sleep."*

I left my body. I don't know where I went. Somewhere far away, somewhere safe. When I found myself back again, the room was empty and Amelia Dyer was gone.

DISSOCIATING

It's called dissociating, leaving your body. When bad things are happening to me, I put myself somewhere far away, and then the bad things can't hurt me. I keep myself there, and when I come back, the bad things are gone.

It's something I learned to do when I lived with Violet, and bad things happened to me a lot. It's not something I can control, it just happens. Sometimes it's useful. Sometimes it's horrible and scary, because you wake up and you don't know where you are, or what just happened, or why everyone is looking at you like you're crazy. I hate it, because not being in control is one of my worst, worst things, and it's bad enough not being in control of other people, but when you're not in control of your own head, it's terrifying. But sometimes being in my body is even worse, so I understand why my head does it.

It's sort of a superpower, but a horrible one.

One of the few things my stupid therapist Helen could do was deal with dissociation. She used to hold my hand and rub my skin, and talk to me in this calm voice, just reminding me over and over of where I was, and that I was safe. Liz was good at it too. But the problem with moving so much was that new people had to learn everything over again, and sometimes people forgot to tell them things, and then they didn't know what to do.

I wasn't sure if Jim knew about dissociating or not. It scared me, that something so big and scary might happen at any time, and he wouldn't know how to deal with it.

KNIFE

The next day at school, I stole the biggest knife I could find from the cookery corner and put it in my school rucksack.

When I got home, I hid the knife in my big pencil case and hid the pencil case at the very back of my bedside cabinet. Then I felt better.

I knew that lady was old Amelia. I knew she was dangerous.

If she came back, I'd be ready.

HOME NUMBER 10
VIOLET

I moved in with Violet after my first set of adoptive parents dumped me. I was nearly seven. It was the first house I'd ever lived in without Hayley. I was furious about that. I screamed at my social worker, "You can't split me and Hayley up! She's my sister!"

My worker didn't look that much older than some of the big kids in foster care. She had a pale blue cardigan, and brown hair that she kept tucking behind her ears. She looked terrified when I started screaming at her.

"Look," she said, "Hayley's got a mummy and daddy now—"

"They're *my* mummy and daddy," I howled. Hayley and me had been living with them for ages. I called them Mummy and Daddy. They told us they were going to be our parents for ever and ever.

"I know—" she said, and she stopped. "But they can't – I mean, they want very much to stay in touch, but. . . Look, this is a nice family for Hayley. Surely you can be happy for her?"

"They're not nice," I said. "They're horrible!" And I spat in her face, brown pity-chocolate spit that dripped down her nose and on to her little-kid cardigan.

It didn't do any good, all my shouting. They still took me away. And then they put me with Violet.

Violet was the worst foster mother I ever lived with. I hated her. *Hated* her.

She had loads of kids: three teenage kids of her own and three foster kids. People were always saying how looking after all those kids must be a lot of work, but it wasn't because we all had to do chores for her, plus whenever we were bad, we did housework as punishment. I was really little when I lived there, but I still had to do drying up and hoovering and tidying. I was the littlest kid there – the others were teenagers. They were scary. They would come into my bedroom when I was asleep, and hide bottles in my wardrobe or just mess with my head, sticking matches between my toes and then lighting them, seeing how long it took me to wake up. I used to stay awake for as long as I could, but I always had to fall asleep in the end. I shared my room with this other girl, but if she woke up when the other kids came in, she wouldn't wake me. She'd just let them get on with it, and be pleased that they were picking on me instead of her.

Violet was no help. If you told on the other kids she'd say, "Nobody loves a tattle-tale!" And then she made you go and hoover the living room.

When I was bad at my mum's house, she used to lock me in the cupboard. Violet used to lock us in the cellar. Once, when I'd just moved there and was screaming because I missed Hayley so much, she locked me in the cellar for hours and hours and hours. It was the worst thing that's ever happened to me, much worse than anything my mum ever did. It was black, black, black, and I felt like I couldn't breathe. I thought she'd forgotten about me and I was never going to get out and I was going to die in there. I screamed and screamed, and hammered on the door until my hands bled, but she didn't let me out.

Sometimes, she used to make me stand in the shower while one of the others kept the water on freezing cold. Other times she used to make me stand on one leg in the corner. If I touched the walls, or put my foot down, I had to stay there for longer. She'd sit at the table, laughing away with one of her kids, and I'd just have to stand there.

Violet's was the first foster home I ever lived in with lots of kids. I hated almost everything about it. I hated how the fridge and all the cupboards in the kitchen were kept locked, so you couldn't steal food. I hated how if you needed something, there were always four or five other kids who wanted something first, and half the time what you needed got forgotten. I hated being the smallest, the one all the other kids picked on when they were bored. I was afraid all the time, living with Violet. I wanted to run away, but I was only little, and I knew that if I did they'd just find me and take me straight back. I tried everything I could to be good. I kept my mouth shut and never said anything except when someone asked me a question. I stopped throwing tantrums. Usually when I'm afraid it turns into angry, but in Violet's house the scared was too big, and it just stayed scared. I never even cried, 'cause it used to annoy the girl I shared a room with, and she'd come and punch me in the stomach, hard, to shut me up.

Violet's house was when I first started leaving my body. I'd be standing in the shower, cold water pouring off me, and I'd just go. Sometimes it would be like I was outside my body, watching myself. Sometimes everything would go black. Sometimes I'd still be there, but distant, as though the bad things were happening to someone else, and I'd feel nothing. At first I liked it, but then it got scary because it would happen at school, or when I was supposed to be hoovering or something, and I wouldn't be able to stop it.

I lived with Violet from the summer I was seven till the middle of the next spring. Eventually, one of the big kids got a phone with a video recorder on it, and recorded Violet locking this other kid in the cellar.

And only then did they take us away.

THE GREAT WAR OF OLIVIA'S BEDTIME

After that first time, Amelia started coming into my room pretty regularly. At the start, it was just every couple of nights. That was bad enough, though.

I fought back, of course. I always fight. Jim called it the Great War of Olivia's Bedtime. Daniel called it Olivia Being a Drama Queen, but only once. After I nearly bashed his nose in, he stopped.

I called it Survival At All Costs.

I refused to go to bed. I invented headaches and spiders in my room *RIGHT THERE! THERE! CAN'T YOU SEE IT?* and last-minute homework. I lost urgent, important things that had to be found *right now this minute*. All my pyjamas mysteriously vanished, and when Jim lent me T-shirts to sleep in, they vanished too. He must have bought about fifty toothbrushes, because I kept dropping them in muddy puddles or shoving them into the bottom of the compost bin; everybody's toothbrush, not just mine, so he couldn't just say that having rotten teeth was my own stupid fault. In the end, he kept them locked up and delivered them to us one by one like lollipops. I never brushed my teeth, though. Or got undressed. I wet the bed, deliberately, so the sheets had to be changed. I *screamed* as soon as the light was turned out, on and on and on, until Maisy woke up and started wailing, and Grace shouted at me to, "Shut up right *now*, you little snot."

I never minded being shouted at. I would have ripped my room to shreds if it meant I didn't have to go to bed, except the first time I tried that, Jim just shut the door and left me to it, and being alone is my *worst* thing, after Amelia. The whole point was to get Jim to *stay*, not leave. Or – even better – for me not to have to go to bed at all. I don't need sleep. Grown-ups stay up half the night drinking and watching telly and smooching, and if they can do it, so can I.

Jim tried to talk to me about it. He tried a lot. I even told him the truth, after I realized the spiders and the headaches weren't going to work. I told everyone the truth, but no one believed me. Well, Harriet did, but she was the only one. Helen thought I was making the whole thing up. Daniel didn't say very much, but he frowned and made ghosts-aren't-real-Olivia faces. Liz actually laughed at me. She really did.

"It's an old house, Olivia! It makes funny noises at night. That's what old houses do."

"It's not just *noises*," I said. "It's a *ghost*. She comes into my room at night and *sings*."

"Sounds like a nightmare to me," said Liz. I wanted to punch her. Just because I used to tell stupid lies when I lived with her, she didn't believe me when a real genuine Victorian murderess from beyond the grave was coming to get me!

"It *wasn't* a nightmare," I said. "It *wasn't*. It was *real*."

Liz sighed. "Look, Olivia," she said. "Sometimes you get confused between what's real and what isn't. Like the time you thought your mum had broken into the house and was going to kidnap you, remember? Or the time I was late picking you up from swimming, and you thought I didn't want to be your foster mum any more, and I was just going to leave you there. Just because something feels like it's happening, doesn't mean it is. Remember?"

But Amelia wasn't like those things. Amelia was real.

Jim listened best out of all of the grown-ups.

"Old Amelia comes and visits me," I told him, the first time he asked me why I didn't want to go to bed. "And she's evil. I don't know why she keeps haunting me, but I bet she wants to possess me and make me do something awful, like she did to those other girls. She *hates* me."

Jim didn't even blink.

"OK," he said. "So what would you like me to do about it?"

"I want to sleep in your room," I said. "Or Daniel's room. I don't want to sleep on my own."

"No way!" said Daniel.

Jim rubbed his eyes. "Olivia, you can't sleep in my room. You know they have rules about that. I'm sorry, but Social Services aren't going to change their mind on that one. And it's great that you and Daniel get on so well, but he needs his own space. How would you fit into his room, anyway?"

"We could have bunk beds!" I said. "And I don't need a desk! I could just pile my clothes on top of the chest of drawers. I don't have that much stuff."

"No!" said Daniel. "Seriously, Dad. No."

"No," said Jim. "Not going to happen. Come on, Olivia, help me out here. Give me something I can work on."

"We could move house," I said hopefully, but he wouldn't do that either.

"*I WON'T!*" I screamed, night after night after night. I jumped up and down on the sofa, bouncing as high as I could, screaming, "*I WON'T! I WON'T!*"

"Dad—" said Harriet, clinging to Jim's hand like the little kid she was.

"Make her *stop* before she wakes the baby," said Grace.

Jim sighed and pulled his hand down his face, stretching the skin so he looked old and tired. "Better in a family with kids, eh?" he said. "I hope you know what you're talking about, Liz Bishop."

He said it under his breath, like he thought I couldn't hear him. He didn't know about my supersonic hearing. My stomach clenched so tight I thought I was going to be sick. Liz never looked tired, or like she couldn't cope; it was one of the best things about her.

He doesn't want me. I knew he didn't.

I spat right in his face.

If I scream loud enough, he can't leave me.

In the end, we came to a sort of compromise. Jim would put Harriet to bed, then me. He even managed to get me to brush my teeth, which he did through a very sneaky, Liz-ish trick. He told me I didn't have to brush them, but if I wasn't going to look after my teeth, I couldn't have sweet things. Then he served ice cream and chocolate cake for pudding every night for a week.

When I lived with Liz, I had this Batman night light for when I was afraid of the dark. It got left behind when I moved because I refused to pack any of the presents she'd given me, and I didn't need it at Fairfields, because my door had a window on top of it into the corridor where the light was always left on. Liz brought the night light over one Saturday, which helped a bit, but mostly because having it in my room at night reminded me of Liz, and Liz always made me feel safe.

When I was in bed, Jim would come and sit beside me until I fell asleep. At first he just sat there, but after a while he got fed up of me trying to make him talk, so he started reading to me instead. I liked that. I liked pretending that I was little, and Jim was my dad reading to me before bed. I used to close my eyes really tight and pretend that nothing could get me, because my dad was there. I pretended that he loved me. I pretended I was safe. I pretended that when I woke up in the night, he wouldn't be gone.

NIGHT-TIME VISITORS

But he did go. And when he went, Amelia came.

Some nights I didn't think she was going to come at all. It was only later that she came every night. At first it was maybe a couple of times a week. But I never knew if she was coming or not.

One problem with supersonic hearing was that whenever Maisy woke up and started crying, I'd wake up too. I hate the noise babies make when they cry. I hated it when it was Maisy and I hated it when it was weird ghost babies, and I hated it *most of all* when it was in the middle of the night and I didn't know whether it was ghost crying or real crying. Maisy – or the Victorian baby, whichever it was – used to get muddled in my head with my brother, Jamie. He used to cry like that, on and on and on.

When I heard the baby crying, it would sort of time-machine me back to being little again. That's another superpower, I suppose, travelling in time, but it's more like a curse than a power. It's not like I can zip into the future or anything. My brain just zaps me back into my most horrible memories with no warning, and there's nothing I can do to stop it.

I'd be there in bed, listening to the baby crying, and then—

I'm at my mum's house, and Jamie's crying, and—

"Go to sleep, my baby, close your pretty eyes. . ."

Amelia's there, rocking Jamie, and—

And I'd be back in Jim's house, terrified, because if Amelia could get into my past, then where would I ever be safe? I'd get so angry at Maisy for crying and setting her off. I'd think *Shut up, Maisy. Please, please, shut up. Shut up or I'll kill you.* And then I'd remember that that was what my mum used to say to Jamie, and that would scare me even more. I want to be like Liz when I grow up, happy and strong, not angry and crazy and sad like my mum.

I'd sit there on the bed, listening, trying to work out if Amelia was there or not. I never saw her. But I *heard* her, and that was nearly as bad. She had a peculiar, particularly horrible smell: tobacco, and alcohol, and milk, and sweat, and dust, and old, dry skin. She smelled of old person; old person who didn't wash. And she smelled of fear; my fear.

She'd come up to the bed. I'd *feel* her hand against my cheek. That would be enough by itself to flash me back into the past, to my mum's hand, just like that, stroking my cheek before she hit me. I'd be five, and then I'd be eleven, and then my mum would be there, and then Amelia would be there, and then I'd be in Violet's cellar, and then I'd be alone, and everything would get muddled in my head, and I'd want to weep, but I was too scared even to scream.

Afterwards, I'd sit on my bed, half dead with terror. Leaving the room was awful, but staying was even worse, so at last I'd get out of bed and run down the corridor to the light switch. Once the light was on, I'd run to Jim's room and crawl into his bed.

If Jim woke up when I came in, he'd send me back to my room. Luckily he had this big double bed, so if I brought my own duvet and crept in quietly, then sometimes I could sleep in the far corner and he wouldn't know until morning. Well, it worked twice. Usually he woke up, and then he'd take me back to bed. The first time he tried that, I screamed and screamed and screamed so loudly that I woke up everyone in the house. Maisy started wailing, and Grace threatened to chop off my head and mash it into a billion pieces and feed it to Pork Scratchings.

Jim used to sit with me in the night as well, but in the middle of the night, after a visit from Amelia, I was so scared that I probably wasn't going to go to sleep again *ever*, so Jim would just sit there reading chapter after chapter, while I lay back, wide awake and only slightly less frightened than I was before he came, because I knew he was itching to go back to sleep and leave me on my own with Amelia. Whenever he looked like stopping, I only had to open my mouth to start screaming and he'd pick up the book again. I sort of liked that I could get him to do what I wanted, and I sort of didn't, because the sort of dad who can be outsmarted by an eleven-year-old probably isn't smart enough to protect me from all the people I need protecting from. So that made me sad, and it made me even more sure that I wouldn't be staying here for long.

One night, I stayed awake for four and a half hours, while he read eight chapters of some stupid book about wizards and eventually fell asleep on my bedside chair while trying to Relax me with a Relaxation CD.

"Are you going to make him stay up *every* night?" said Daniel, while we made ourselves porridge with chocolate sprinkles and marshmallows for breakfast.

"If I have to," I said.

"You can borrow Zig-Zag if you like," said Daniel. Zig-Zag usually slept on Daniel's bed, but he didn't know how to work door handles, so it wasn't hard to persuade him to sleep somewhere else. "Cats can see ghosts. Or they can in Discworld anyway."

"Really?" I said. I was pretty surprised.

"Sure," said Daniel. He tipped the hundreds and thousands tub upside down into his bowl. Hundreds and thousands poured out, covering the porridge and half the table. "Oops. Hey, let me know if he sees anything."

"Bet he will," I said.

*

I like animals. People always think I'm going to beat them up, but I never do. Animals don't care if you don't do your homework, or have screaming fits, or tell lies, or are visited by ghosts. If you play with them and give them biscuits, animals love you for ever.

If only humans were so easy.

Zig-Zag curled up happily at the end of my bed. Jim came in and read me a chapter. He looked pretty tired.

"You aren't going to wake me up again tonight, are you?" he said.

"I might," I said.

Jim kissed my forehead. "Let's try not to, eh?" he said.

When I woke up, Jim was gone and the light was out in the hall. Zig-Zag was a warm, heavy weight on my feet. I wriggled a bit to see if he was still awake and he went, *Maow?* Daniel was right – I did feel better with him there. I opened my eyes. The room was dimly but clearly lit by the night light. I lay on my back, as still as possible, listening. Somewhere in the house, a baby began to cry. I couldn't tell if it was Maisy or someone long ago. It didn't *sound* like Maisy, but it was hard to be sure.

I sat up in bed, listening, waiting for Amelia to come. I couldn't hear anything, except the baby crying, but the baby made me tense up all over. I wondered if I dared get out of bed and switch the light on, but I was afraid of what might happen to me if I moved.

Zig-Zag padded up the bed and curled up on my lap. He reminded me of Daniel and that made me feel safer. It was a new feeling, liking someone. I hardly ever liked people. Before I came to Jim's I liked Hayley and Liz, and that was it. But now I liked Daniel, and Harriet, and Maisy, and Pork Scratchings, and Zig-Zag, and sometimes Grace, when she was in a good mood, and . . . well, I sort of liked Jim. Sometimes. Maybe.

Thinking of all the people I liked made me feel a little calmer. I picked up Zig-Zag and went into Daniel's room. He was lying asleep on his back, his mouth slightly open. There was a thin cake-slice of moonlight shining through the curtains and on to his face.

Just being in the same room as Daniel made me feel safer. I climbed into his bed and pushed him over to the other side to make room. He groaned. "What are you doing?"

"I'm coming in with you," I said.

Daniel moaned. "What's wrong with your own bed?"

"There's evil things."

I expected him to tell me to get lost, but he just groaned again, rolled over and went straight back to sleep.

There was hardly space for the two of us in the bed, but it was so much safer with Daniel there that I didn't care. I stayed awake for ages, expecting Amelia to come, but she didn't, so I guess she wasn't as powerful as Daniel. If I was a Ghostbuster, I'd make Essence of Daniel and sell it to people in haunted houses, to keep them safe for ever.

MUMMY AND DADDY

Mummy and Daddy were the first family who nearly adopted me. I was six. My sister Hayley was just four.

I thought being adopted was going to be great, at first. Our new mummy and daddy came and visited us at the foster home we were living in. They spent a whole week taking us to theme parks, and bowling, and shopping for duvet covers and towels and pictures for our bedroom. It was brilliant. I thought being adopted meant we would spend all day doing fun stuff and getting bought whatever we asked for by these people who thought we were wonderful.

Our new mummy and daddy had loads of money. They had this house with four bedrooms – one for them, me, Hayley and their kid Ben, who was a couple of years older than me. Ben had his own bike, a scooter, a trampoline, a Nintendo, a skateboard, roller skates, and about three hundred bits of Lego.

"Do we get that many toys, now we live here?" I said.

And we nearly did. All Mummy and Daddy's friends came to visit and they all bought us stuff. They thought we were super cute. Hayley *was* super cute, of course, and I got very good at pretending to be. I used to put my head on one side, and lisp, "Fwank you, Gwanny," like I didn't know how to speak properly. My old foster mum Donna used to pretend not to hear me if I spoke like that to her, but Mummy and Daddy's friends thought it was adorable. I learned loads of ways to get them to buy me stuff. There was one day we went to the pantomime, and I got Mummy, Daddy, Granny and Uncle Something-Or-Other each to buy me a family bag of Maltesers. I hid them under my coat, and Hayley and I ate them all through the show. We weren't half sick afterwards, but it was worth it.

When I first moved in, I was very, very, very good. I was terrified that if they found out how bad I was in real life, they'd get rid of me, so I did everything I could to act like the sort of nice little girl they wanted. I called them Mummy and Daddy. I let them hug me and kiss me sloppy goodnight kisses. I pretended like I cared about all the dolls and Barbies and Sylvanians and board games and story books they bought me. They were a weird family about toys. Their kid Ben had loads of Playmobil and action figures, and he used to spend hours moving them pointlessly around on the floor.

"Darth Vader's attacking! *Zzzung! Zzzung!* Batman to the rescue! Everyone in the Batmobile! *Neeeeooooww!* I'm going to kill you!"

Mummy and Daddy thought this was cute instead of weird. They used to join in Ben's games, and when we were out they used to try and make us play too.

"Careful on the stepping stones," they'd say. "Or you'll get eaten by alligators!"

When I first met them, I didn't realize they were kidding. I thought we really *were* going to get eaten by alligators, and I couldn't understand why everyone looked so cheerful about it. When I figured it out, I got pretty annoyed. Here I was working hard to keep Hayley and me safe, playing nice so they didn't dump us, watching and listening all the time, so when they started hitting us, I wouldn't be taken by surprise. And they'd had me wasting my time worrying about alligators and Darth Vader.

It was hard pretending to be nice all the time. Mummy and Daddy obviously wanted some perfect little kid like Ben, who never got angry or rude like I did. Every time they gave me another stupid doll, or told me I was clever, or beautiful, or wonderful, it would remind me how ugly and bad I really was, if only they knew. I'd feel this rumbly, grumbly, stomach-eating anger bubbling up inside me, and the only way I could keep it from getting out and eating Mummy and Daddy's happy family was to poke pencils into their cat, or stab scissors in their pillows, or tear all their money into bits and throw it away.

Everything they did reminded me of the good little girl

they wanted and I wasn't. I had this yucky pink-and-white bedroom with white furniture and a shelf of books I never read, and a little white dressing-table. I hated that room. I'd never slept in a different bedroom from Hayley before, and I used to creep in with her at night after Mummy and Daddy had put us to bed.

At first, Mummy and Daddy hardly got cross with us at all. But after we'd been there a couple of months, they started to get strict. It was all "No, you can't take food without asking" (which was stupid 'cause if you asked, they just said no) and "No, you can't draw on the walls" (why not? It was *my* room) and "Don't boss Ben around, let him choose" (which was even stupider, because Ben didn't have two brain cells to rub together and he always picked stupid games that I didn't understand, and anyway, I had more practice at being a big sister than he had being a big brother. I *always* picked what we played when we lived with Mum).

Also, they started trying to come between me and Hayley, which was totally not fair because Hayley was *my* sister first. *I* was the one who looked after her. They adored Hayley, and they always wanted to be the ones to brush her hair, and wash her face, and give her a hug when she was crying, and do all the things that were *my* job. *And* Hayley used to let them. I told her not to, but then she'd start to cry, and I'd get told off, which was stupid because *they'd* started it.

They were really bossy. They wouldn't let me be in charge of *anything*. I had to wear a manky school uniform

128

every school day, even though the jumper made my skin itch. They made me eat all their yucky dinners, and hold their hands when we walked down the street (even though I'd been walking down stupid streets on my own for *years*) and always do exactly what they said exactly when they said it Right Now And No Arguing, otherwise they'd stick me on the sofa on my own and not talk to me.

Some of the time, I didn't even realize I *was* being bad. Like lying. Mum told lies all the time, and she used to get me and Hayley to tell them too.

"Mummy isn't here," when the police came round.

"I've lost my mummy," to distract the shop people while she went shoplifting. And, "I don't *know*," when teachers asked where I'd got all those burns and bruises.

Mum really liked me when I told lies, but my new mummy and daddy hated it.

When they told me I was bad, I'd get frightened, because then I knew they were going to dump me. And when I get frightened, I get angry, and when I get angry, I *have* to do something. I can't just *stop* being angry, can I? So I'd smash their stupid plates, and kick their stupid spoilt cat, or punch Idiot Ben until his nose bled, and they'd be all, "You can't behave like this, Olivia," and I'd just look at them and not understand. Because this is who I *am*– I can't do anything about it. I can't stop being angry, or missing my mum, or loving Hayley, or wetting the bed, or being afraid of the dark, or not loving my new mummy and daddy, or getting hungry and nicking food, or any of the other things people dump you for. I don't *try* and get scared and angry. I was just born like this.

And that's why nobody will ever want me.

PLAYING HOME

I was kind of surprised when I realized all the things I liked about living with the Iveys. I liked that Daniel and Harriet were my friends. I never had a proper friend before I came to live with Jim. I had Hayley, but she was my sister. I had the big girls who liked to dress me up like a doll when I lived in Fairfields, but they weren't friends either. Liz kept trying to introduce me to kids she thought I might like, but it never worked. They liked me for a bit, and then they stopped.

"You're my friend, aren't you?" I said to Daniel. "*Aren't you?*"

"Course I am," said Daniel. He looked a bit surprised that I even had to ask.

"You don't think I'm bonkers?"

"*Of course* I think you're bonkers," said Daniel. "That doesn't mean we're not friends!"

My stupid therapist Helen practically peed her pants when I told her about Daniel and Harriet. You'd think I'd single-handedly defeated a Dalek invasion or something.

"And you like these children?" she said.

"No," I said. "They're stupid." But it wasn't true. I liked them both.

I liked that Harriet was so much younger than me. I liked that I got to look after her, because mostly my life was other people trying to look after me. I liked that with Harriet I didn't have to pretend to be bigger and tougher than I really was. I could play baby games and nobody cared.

My favourite game to play with Harriet was building dens. The farm was a great place for dens. We started off making hay-houses in the barn. Then we discovered you could build dens in the hedges. Lots of the hedges had holes in them already, nearly big enough to crawl into. I used to borrow Jim's hedge-cutters to make the holes big enough to live in.

After a bit, we started to notice all the crates and pallets and bits of old wood lying around the farmyard. I wanted to make a tree house in one of the apple trees in the orchard, but it turned out that tree houses are hard. You have to spend ages just banging nails into branches. The floor was OK, but the walls were awful. You could either use pallets (which had all these long holes in them, so the wind blew through) or you had to make do with old

132

bits of wood, all different sizes and none of them strong enough to hold a roof.

"You've got gun slits," said Daniel. He got interested once we started using a hammer and nails. "*Pow! Pow! Pow!*" He pretended to shoot a revolver through the holes in one of the pallets.

"I don't want a house with *holes* in it!" I said.

Daniel liked the building bit best. Harriet liked the arranging – bringing out pillows and curtains and dolls' tea sets and cake and all the things we might need if we really lived here.

What I liked best was the last bit, when the den was done. I liked it when we pulled the roof on over the top – sometimes a board of wood, but usually just an old curtain or blanket. I liked having walls and a roof on all sides of me. I liked the feeling you got inside. *This is my house. No one can get in.*

Another thing I liked about living with the Iveys was how much space there was. Daniel and I used to ride our bikes into the woods, or round the farmyard, or down the hill in the pig field, *bump, bump, bump* until one of us fell off. I liked doing tricks on the scooters in the barn, and the ping-pong table, and making dams, and having water fights in the beck, and riding our bikes through the water so it splashed up all around us, and leaping off the hayloft on to the bales below shouting, "Geronimo!" and "I *kiiill* you!" and other stupid things like that.

I liked stealing Daniel's books to read. Dopey Graham and Grumpy Annabel were always trying to get me to read, and I used to pretend like I couldn't just to wind them up. But Jim didn't care if I read or not, so I didn't mind doing it in his house. Daniel had loads of comics – *Batman*, and old *Doctor Who* annuals, and *X-Men*, and a whole box of *Beano*s, and half a shelf of *Asterix* books which were falling to bits, they were so old. I think they used to belong to Jim when *he* was a kid. I loved Asterix. He made me laugh so much, him and Obelix, and Cacofonix the bard, and Vitalstatistix the chief, who got carried around the village by his servants on a shield. When I played Asterix with Harriet and Daniel I wanted to be Vitalstatistix and get carried around, but Daniel and Harriet wouldn't. I tried to explain that it was *realistic*, that the real Vitalstatistix was much heavier than me, and if *his* servants could do it, so should they. Especially if Daniel was going to be Asterix. But Harriet said she was going to be Dogmatix, because she liked dogs, and dogs didn't carry people, and Daniel said Asterix didn't carry people either. No one wanted to be the Romans, so it was a bit of a stupid game. You need people to beat up in games.

Doctor Who never worked either, because Daniel and I just used to fight over who got to be the Doctor. Liz suggested that one of us could be a Doctor from the past and the other a Doctor from the future, but Harriet got fed up of always being the monsters. She said it wasn't fair, because whenever she killed us we regenerated into a new Doctor, but when we killed her she stayed dead. She wanted to be the Doctor's new companion, Harriet, but then we had no one to blow up. Except when Liz came round. Liz could do all the aliens, with voices and everything.

Sometimes I think Harriet got muddled between what was real and what was pretend. For example, she always treated Amelia Dyer like she was a baddie in a pretend game.

"I bet Amelia *did* murder babies here," she said. "She was a baby farmer! That's what she did! Just because no one ever found any bodies. I bet there are babies buried *right here* in the garden. Let's see if we can find them!"

Harriet had very definite ideas about where the bodies might be buried. Jim had a file of papers about the history of the house, and apparently when Amelia Dyer lived here, the fields were all rented out, like they were now. There were several photographs of our fields all full of corn, with dopey-looking farm boys pushing ploughs.

"She couldn't have buried the babies in the fields," Harriet said. "That's what Dad says. She'd have had to dig up the corn! And the yard would have been full of farm people and dogs and stuff. So *I* think she buried them in the garden."

Personally, I thought Jim just didn't want Harriet to dig up other people's fields. But he kind of had a point too.

Jim's file had a photocopy of a picture of Amelia Dyer's garden, drawn by the woman who lived here after she did. Harriet spent ages looking at this picture, trying to work out where Amelia might have buried her babies. She reckoned it was the creepy flower beds at the bottom of the garden, where the old fountain was, because that was the one place in the picture where there wasn't grass or flowers. She wanted us to go and start digging for corpses, but neither Daniel or I wanted to. Daniel thought the whole thing was bonkers. And the bottom of the garden still scared me. It reminded me of the hidden places in the garden at Fairfields, where the big kids used to go to drink and smoke and take drugs.

Plus, whenever I went down there, I felt like Amelia was watching me.

Sometimes Daniel played with me and Harriet, and sometimes he wanted to stay in and draw or read. He was always reading, real books, without pictures. I liked stories, but I didn't like real books. They're like a test, and what book you read is what mark you get. Daniel scored high, because he read grown-up books like Discworld, but I liked books like *Where's Wally?* which is about a zero because it doesn't have any words in it. I didn't like scoring zero, so I just never read books without pictures, and then they couldn't judge me.

It made me scared, all the things I liked, because I knew I couldn't stay for ever, and that made me angry. I didn't want to like things so much, and care when they were gone, so then I had to find things to do to show that I didn't care. Like one time, I pulled Daniel's copy of *Asterix and the Big Fight* apart and scribbled on the torn-up pages in black felt tip and left them lying about. Jim made me wash up every night for a week to earn the money to replace it, but the new book was all smooth-shiny new, and I knew Daniel didn't like it as much as the dog-eared copy that used to belong to his dad.

MOTHERS

The last time I saw my mum was just before I was adopted for the first time. I was six. Hayley and I were taken to visit her in this little office in Children's Services. There was a desk with someone else's family photos on it, and low chairs to sit on. Our social worker was there too. It wasn't Carole; it was an old one. I've forgotten her name.

I don't remember very much about the meeting, except it was weird. Hayley and I got shy and didn't know what to say, and I think my mum got shy too. She gave us presents, I remember that. Hayley got a pink fairy doll's house, and I got a stupid plastic doll with ringlets. I remember being jealous of Hayley, because her present was so much better, and also a bit suspicious of my doll, because my mum had never given me a present before. Hayley got presents sometimes, but I never did. So I remembered wondering if my doll was really from my mum, or from someone else, and if this person who looked like my mum really *was* her, or if maybe the doll was a trap. Like, if I didn't like it, I'd get told off for being ungrateful, and if I liked it, it would get taken off me next time I was bad, or my mum would tell me it was just a joke and the doll wasn't mine after all. Then she'd give it to Hayley and hit me for playing with Hayley's toys. So I didn't know what to do with it and I remember sort of keeping one hand on the box, but not opening it, thinking that that might sort of count as liking and not liking it. Nothing bad happened to me, though. My mum was more interested in playing with Hayley. After she'd given me the doll, she pretty much ignored me.

Mothers are supposed to love you for ever. They're supposed to look after you, and help you out when you're in trouble, but my mother wasn't like that. She was supposed to stay in touch with us after we got adopted, to send us letters and photographs, but she never did. After that meeting, she just disappeared.

I never stopped thinking about her, though. I never stopped wondering where she was, and if she was all right. I know she was a grown-up, but when I lived with her she often wasn't all right. Often we didn't have enough to eat, or enough money to pay the electricity people to keep us warm. Sometimes, when she'd drunk too much, she'd get sick. Even after six years, I still felt guilty for having a warm bed and enough to eat, when maybe she didn't. If I'd known where she lived, I'd have sent her money. If I had any money.

I wondered if she missed me. Perhaps, after she'd gone away, she'd realized that she'd made a mistake and she loved me after all. I wondered if she was sad, all on her own, or if she had other kids now, if I had little brothers and sisters somewhere, and if she loved them. Perhaps that was why she hadn't got in touch with Social Services, so her new kids wouldn't get taken off her. Or perhaps she was dead. I hoped she wasn't dead.

Sometimes, when I was in Bristol, at the swimming baths, or the pantomime, or anywhere with lots of people, I'd start thinking, *What if my mum's here?* I'd look at the faces of all the women, trying to see if one of them was her. I'd imagine what would happen if she saw me. Would she be happy? Sad? Sometimes I imagined that she'd give me a big hug and tell me she loved me. Sometimes she'd start shouting at me and calling me evil and telling me she wished I was dead. Sometimes she grabbed me and tried to steal me away. Those were the most frightening imaginings. I still looked for her, though. And all the time I was looking, I still hoped I'd find her.

AMELIA AND THE BABY

In Jim's house, things were getting worse. Amelia was coming more and more often, and each time she came, she was scarier than before. I was tired of being watchful all the time, which made me angry, which meant I yelled at Harriet and called her stupid, and Harriet started to cry, and then I got told off, and then I started worrying that Jim, and Harriet, and probably even Daniel didn't like me, and I wondered how long I was going to be able to stay here.

I knew it wouldn't be for long. Amelia was going to make something awful happen and ruin everything. She was totally evil. She hated me, and she hated Maisy even more, I was sure of it. She always seemed to come when Maisy was crying. Like the day Daniel was trying to teach me to ride a unicycle, and I kept falling off, and he could

141

do it no problem, and I yelled at him, and called him stupid again, and—

And Maisy was crying because Grace was trying to put her in the car seat, which she hated. It took me totally by surprise, because I hadn't expected Maisy to be in the yard. I froze. I got stuck in Maisy's crying.

"Stop it!" I shouted.

"I'll smash your face in if you don't shut up," says my mum, and Jamie doesn't stop crying, and I'm terrified, because she's off-her-face drunk, and maybe she'll actually do it. . .

"Make her stop!" I yelled. I clenched my fists together, so tightly that my knuckles went white. "I'll smash her face in, if she doesn't shut up! I will!"

"Olivia!" said Daniel, behind me.

"Give him to me, the poppet," says Amelia. I feel the air move as she passes behind me, so close that I could reach out and touch the fabric of her skirt.

HOME NUMBER 8

DONNA AND CRAIG

Before Hayley got adopted and I got nearly adopted, we lived with these foster parents called Donna and Craig. I was five when we moved in, and we stayed there for nearly a year, which was the longest I'd ever lived in one place ever, even when we lived with my mum. I had to go to school every day, which I liked because we always got food and because I was totally the boss of the teachers. If I didn't like a lesson, I'd just get up and walk out. And if they tried to stop me, I'd scream at the top of my voice. Then I got to go and sit in a quiet place, and not do maths or writing. It was great.

My foster mother Donna was big and rough, and she pulled my hair when she brushed it, but she wasn't mean. She didn't let you mess her about. When she said "No", she meant no. When I kicked her in the shins, she swore at me and said, "If you don't behave, little madam, you're out on your ear." But when she bought something for her own kids, she always bought something for me and Hayley too. She didn't care that I wanted to sleep in the same bed as Hayley. She baked me my first ever birthday cake, *and* she bought me a bike as a birthday present. It was a second-hand bike, but still.

I thought for ages that we were just going to live with Donna and Craig for a bit, then go back to my mum like usually happened. But then one day a social worker came to see us, and she told us that we wouldn't be going back home again, and they were going to find a lovely new family for us to live with.

"What about my mum?" I said. Donna and Craig were all right, but they weren't my mum. And this wasn't my house. There were lots of things I didn't like or understand about it, like bedtimes, and vegetables, and how we'd been there four months and they hadn't hit me or Hayley yet, which meant I never knew when they were going to start, and what might set them off, and I had to be on guard all the time, so I'd know. And I was worried about my brother Jamie – they'd told me he was living with a new family, but I didn't know where he was, or if the new family was looking after him properly. I missed him, and my mum, and staying up all night playing houses with Hayley, and Happy Meals from McDonald's, and how special it was when my mum said she loved me. Donna and Craig's house smelled weird. It never felt like home. And though I was afraid of going back to my mum, at least there I knew who I was, and nobody expected me to brush my teeth, or not swear, or know how to read.

"Your mummy can't look after you properly," said the social worker. "That's why we're going to find you a nice new family you can live with for ever."

"Can't we live here?" I said.

"Donna and Craig just look after children for a little while," said the social worker. "We want to find some people who'll be your family for the rest of your life."

Well, that was a lie. Donna and Craig had two forever children already – their own kid, and a boy with autism they'd adopted, called Lewis. They just didn't want me and Hayley. Or probably they just didn't want me. Hayley was way more good than I was. Probably they just didn't like me, and knowing that made me hate them a bit, because there's nothing worse than being bossed about by someone who doesn't like you, and not being able to escape.

"I don't care," I said. "I wouldn't want to live with them anyway." But it wasn't true.

THE TUESDAY MOON

And as if Amelia wasn't enough to deal with, I *still* had to go to school.

School was boring. The other kids did work. I didn't. I didn't get why anyone would spend all day letting some stupid lady boss them about, making them learn stupid numbers off by heart. I never did. I just wailed and moaned and told her it was too hard, and made such a fuss she was pleased when I stopped complaining and spent the lesson drawing pictures instead.

Harriet still hadn't found any better friends. I worried about that a bit, because what would she do when I was gone? I tried to explain this to her, but she didn't get it.

"You aren't *going* anywhere, Olivia," she said. "You're going to live with us for ever."

"Yeah, until your dad chucks me out," I said. "And

even if I did stay – which I won't – I'll be in Big School next year. So you have to stop letting them boss you about. Or get better friends."

Not that I could talk. No one wanted to be friends with me. It didn't matter though, because I didn't need friends. At break time, I played football with the boys. I was good at football. The boys didn't care what sort of shoes you wore, or what magazines you read or what bands you liked, they just cared about whether you could kick a ball or not.

They didn't like me, though. When we had to pick partners in class, they always picked each other instead of me.

I didn't care. There didn't seem much point in making friends. Sometimes when you moved families they paid for a taxi, so you could keep going to your old school, but Jim's house was so far into the middle of nowhere that I knew when I left, I'd have to go somewhere new.

Stupid therapy with Helen was the other thing that happened. Therapy sessions were mostly useless. Helen asked me stupid questions, and I gave her stupid answers. It was none of her *business* what I thought about things. What I thought was *private*.

Helen was mostly OK with this, but sometimes, if I tried really hard, I could see her getting annoyed. One day, after I'd been living with Jim for about five months, I got her really annoyed.

She was asking about flashbacks. Jim had obviously

told her I was having them, because I hadn't. That was a bad sign. It meant he was worrying about me.

"Tell me what happens," she said.

"Nothing," I said. "Nothing happens. Can I draw pictures now?"

"No," said Helen. "Tell me about your flashbacks. How do they make you feel?"

"Happy," I said. "Drunk. Like I'm made of rubber. Like the man in the moon on Tuesdays. The Tuesday Moon."

Helen sucked in her breath. "Do you *like* living like this?" she said.

I shrugged. "I'm *fine*," I said.

"Are you?" said Helen. "When was the last time you slept through the night?"

"I'm being haunted by a Victorian murderess!" I yelled.

"Before that, Olivia."

I didn't say anything. Never, was the answer.

"When was the last time you felt relaxed?"

"I'm not a relaxed sort of person," I said, which was something Grumpy Annabel said about me once. Only she practically spat it.

"Would you like to be?" said Helen. I gave another shrug. Relaxed sounded dangerous. Bad things might come after you and you wouldn't notice, because you'd be too busy being asleep on a beach or something.

"Do you like being scared all the time?" Helen said.

"I'm not scared all the time!" I shouted. "I'm *never* scared!" Helen gave me her I-know-better-than-you-do look. I wanted to punch her.

"I'm fine!" I shouted. "I'm just me. I *like* being me!"

"Do you like the way you live right now?" Helen said calmly. "All these different families?" I didn't even bother answering. Of *course* I didn't like it. But it wasn't my fault if people keep dumping me, was it?

"Do you think," said Helen, "if you felt a bit safer, you might find it easier to make connections with people?"

"It's not *my* fault I don't feel safe!" I said. "People keep chucking me out!"

"Mm-mm," said Helen. What that meant was, *Of course it's your fault. If you were a nice little girl like Harriet, everyone would want to keep you.*

"Olivia," Helen said, "you weren't born like this. All these problems . . . flashbacks, dissociating, hyper-vigilance . . . they're just symptoms. Your body developed them as a way of coping with the situation you lived in when you were little. I know they help you feel safe and that's important, Olivia, but you don't need them any more. They're all things you can change, but you have to do the work. If you just come here every week and glare at me, we aren't going to get anywhere."

I glared at her. Problems! They weren't problems. They were *superpowers*. I wanted to smack her so hard I broke her nose, but I sort of knew she was a bit right too. Helen had said things like this before, but never so clearly. I honestly wasn't sure what I thought. Part of me really, really wanted to be a dopey little girl like Harriet. But the other part of me – the bigger part – knew that I wasn't safe here, not now, not ever. I probably wouldn't be truly safe until I was grown up, and maybe not even then. So how could I possibly relax?

"If you could have any superpower in the world," I asked Liz, that Saturday, "what would it be?"

"Can I have a TARDIS and a sonic screwdriver?" said Liz, which was cheating. Doctor Who is not a superpower.

Harriet said she would do magic like Harry Potter and fly like Mary Poppins. I told her she could only pick one, so she said she would do magic, and one of the magics she would do would be flying like Mary Poppins. Daniel said he would fly and be invisible and be super strong.

"That's not one superpower!" I said. "That's three! That's cheating!"

Daniel said in that case he would have the power to grant unlimited wishes to anyone, including himself.

Grace said if Harriet was going to be Harry Potter, she was going to be God.

"Being God is *not* a superpower," I told her. "If you ask for God you get nothing."

Grace said in that case, she would have the power to change "the underlying economic underpinnings of society".

"The what?"

"The way the rich have everything and the poor have nothing. I'd make it so people couldn't earn billions of pounds, and if they did, they'd have to give it away to people who had nothing. I'd magically take the money out of their bank accounts and give it to Amnesty International or someone."

"That's stealing," I said. I didn't think superheroes should steal. Probably.

"Yeah," said Grace. "But how would anyone ever know it was me?"

"They would if they asked me," said Daniel. "I'd have to tell them. Then you'd be screwed."

"No, you wouldn't," said Harriet. "*I'd* save you."

Jim was the only one who took it seriously. He thought for ages, then he said he would have the power to heal people.

"You should have been a doctor if you wanted to heal people!" I said. "Not an IT consultant!"

But Jim said there were already plenty of doctors healing the sort of things doctors healed. "I'd heal the things that don't have real-life cures," he said. "The people who are sad and scared and lost. I'd let them be the people they were meant to be all along."

"Eugh!" I pulled a face. What a yucky superpower!

Jim smiled a little sadly and put his arm around my waist.

"What would you pick then, SuperOlivia?"

"Laser deathrays," I said.

But I wouldn't. I'd pick the ability to make people do whatever I wanted them to. I'd make Jim and Liz love me like a real daughter and adopt me, and Daniel and Harriet like me and do whatever I told them to and never argue, and Violet jump off a big cliff into shark-infested water, and my mum come home and love me like she loved Hayley and Jamie, and Hayley ditch her new mum and dad and be my sister, and no one ever hurt me ever, ever again.

Mine was obviously the best superpower, but I didn't want to say in case someone else stole it. I didn't think it would work if more than one person had it, because what would happen if we wanted the same person to do different things? The universe would probably explode, is what.

HOW DO YOU MAKE SOMEONE LOVE YOU?

School broke up for summer. The long holidays started. Grace stopped stressing about exams and started stressing about exam results, which was nearly as bad.

Jim was going camping in Cornwall for a week. Harriet told me all about it. They went every year, apparently, and there was a beach and a disco and an island with puffins on it. At first, I wasn't sure if I was invited or not, because sometimes foster families dump you in respite when they go on holiday. Apparently I was, though, and so were Grace and Maisy. But before that, there were five long, empty weeks of summer.

Summer frightened me. Islands with puffins on them frightened me. I knew I wouldn't get to keep them.

*

I used to watch Daniel and Jim, trying to work out if they hated me yet and if so, how much. Sometimes, when I was bored, I'd go up to Daniel's room and try and get him to talk to me. Most of the time, he'd come and do things with me, but sometimes he'd be drawing or reading or something, and he wouldn't want to. I couldn't bear it.

"Daniel," I'd say. "Dan-iel. Do you want to come out on your bike?"

"No," Daniel would say, and carry on with whatever he was doing. I'd feel the cold fear sink into the bottom of my stomach.

"Come *on*," I'd say. "Let's play on skateboards. Let's watch a DVD. Let's go and annoy Grace. Let's—"

"Not now," Daniel would say. "I'm reading."

And I'd start to feel sick.

He hates you, but he's too nice to say so. He's always hated you.

Why wouldn't he? *I'd* hate me, if I had to live with me.

I hate being on my own. I told you that, didn't I? I start thinking everyone's forgotten me, and I'll probably just keel over and die of bubonic plague or something. No one will even notice. Or maybe they'll notice how much nicer it is without me and decide they don't want me in their family any more, or they'll suddenly go off on a hot-air balloon ride without me, or take a boat to Africa or something. I'm not just being stupid saying that, either. My mum went off and forgot about us loads of times. And I've been in plenty of foster families who used to dump me in respite care and then go on holiday without me. Sometimes they wouldn't even tell me they were going to do it, either. I'd just get home from school and my bags would be packed and everyone else would be off to Disneyland without me.

So when Daniel and Harriet were busy, I used to go and bug Jim. Jim didn't like me any more than Daniel did, but he had to be polite because he was supposed to be my dad.

This time, Jim was in the kitchen, chopping things.

"What are you making?" I said.

I could see what he was making – spaghetti bolognese. But I wanted him to talk to me.

"What do you think I'm making?" he said.

"Ice cream sundae," I told him.

"That sounds nice," he said. "Maybe you could make us some for pudding?"

"Why should I when you're already making it?" I said, and Jim smiled.

"Of course. Silly me. Is this the sort of sundae you like?"

He was laughing at me. I hate it when people laugh at me.

"Why are you putting mushrooms in ice cream?" I said. If I'd asked Grumpy Annabel something stupid like that, we'd have had this whole argument:

"I'm making spaghetti bolognese."

"No, you're not. That's ice cream."

"It's mince, Olivia!"

"And that's sprinkles."

155

"They're onions! And this is a tin of bloody tomatoes."

But Jim just smiled and said, "What do you think the answer is?"

Stupid Jim pretending to be clever. I didn't say anything.

There was an awful empty silence. Jim went *chop, chop, chop* like I wasn't even there.

"Why do you have that rubbish beard?" I said.

"Why do you think?"

"How should I know? *I* wouldn't have a beard like that if you paid me."

"You'd look a bit silly with a beard," said Jim.

I scowled. "You always look silly," I said. "You look like an idiot. I'd hate to look like you. I'd rather look like a sea monster than look like you. I'd rather be dead!"

Jim didn't answer, but I could smell him readying himself for something bad to happen. He was afraid. Or – not afraid, but wary. Like I was a bad thing he'd rather not deal with.

I *hated* him.

"Why are you so horrible to Dad?" Daniel said. We were sitting in the tree house, legs dangling over the edge. He didn't say it in a mean way. More . . . just curious.

"I'm not horrible!" I said. "He's horrible to *me*! He's the one who's always telling me to go sit in the dining room!"

But I could see Daniel didn't believe me. I didn't believe me either, really. I wanted to explain it properly, so he'd understand and maybe not hate me. But I wasn't sure it made sense to anyone who wasn't me. I didn't think even Daniel – who was about the most understandingest person I'd ever met, after Liz – would get it, and that would prove I really *was* crazy.

What I'd have liked to have said was:

"I don't have power over *anything*. Not where I live, not whether I get to keep my stuff when I move, not who my mum and dad are, not *anything*. And it's horrible. It's . . . like panicking, all the time. So anything I can do to make me feel safe, I do. And having power, being in control of *something*, even if it's just how pissed off Jim is with me, feels safer than feeling like I'm about to sink.

"Because there's nothing in my life that's solid. I don't have a home. I don't have a family. I don't have anyone who loves me. So I have to have something to hold on to, or I'll drown."

Jim didn't love me. I knew he didn't. I watched him, dancing Maisy round the room.

"Row, row, row your boat, gently down the stream. Merrily, merrily, merrily, merrily, life is but a dream."

Maisy swayed from side to side in his arms, dancing along. She looked happy. Happy and loved.

"Why does Grace love Maisy?" I said.

"Because she's her mum," said Jim.

It wasn't a good enough answer. Not all mums love their kids.

"Would Grace still love Maisy if Maisy was evil?" I said. "If she was a killer psycho baby?"

"Babies aren't evil," said Jim. But he was wrong. *I* was an evil baby. I made my mum sick, and screamed all night and threw up over her stuff. She told me about it. Often.

"Maisy's dad doesn't love her," I said. "He's never come and visited, not even once."

"I don't think Maisy's dad is any of your business, do you?" said Jim.

"Yes, he *is*," I said. "Because if Maisy's dad doesn't love her, why does *Grace*?"

"Well," said Jim. "Because when a baby is born, a mother's body releases chemicals which help her love the child. Those same chemicals get released when Grace plays with Maisy, or feeds her, or holds her. And also – well, love is a good thing, Olivia. Grace gets a lot of joy from loving Maisy. Most people want to love, and be loved."

I didn't. I didn't want to love anyone, ever, ever, ever. Love was for wimps. If you loved someone, then when they stopped loving you, they destroyed you. I was never going to love anyone ever again. But I would have liked someone to love me like Grace loved Maisy. If you could make someone love you and never leave you – make sure they never stopped loving you – I'd like that. That's what Maisy and Daniel and Harriet had, I reckoned.

"Do you love me?" I asked Jim.

"Well," he said. "Love takes a while to develop." He tried to put the arm that wasn't holding Maisy around me, but I wriggled away.

"I like you," he said, but I didn't believe him.

"How do you make someone love you?" I said.

"You can't," said Jim. "It's just something that happens. Though not throwing food in their face certainly helps."

Huh.

THE BABY

And then it all went wrong.

Maisy was crying. On and on and on. I couldn't bear it. I yelled, "Shut up! Shut up!"

"Shut your mouth," Grace shouted. "Do you have to deal with her? No? Then shut the hell up."

"Shut the hell up, you little moron. What are you doing here, anyway? Who wants you? Do you know what we do to little creeps like you?"

Someone's hand comes down on my face. Someone's foot punches my stomach. I'm drowning. I'm dying. I can't ever escape.

Somewhere, a baby is crying.

"Why can't you just leave me alone?"

*

A baby was crying.

I was back in the living room. Grace had moved. Before, she was standing in front of me; now she was by the window, holding Maisy. My heart was pounding. I felt it again, that piercing sense of being hated, but I couldn't tell if it was the woman in my memory who was doing the hating, or Amelia, and if she was hating me, or the baby, or both of us. I remembered the women in the stories Harriet had told me. There was the lady who tried to gas her children to death, and the other lady who killed her baby and left it on the doorstep. Was that what Amelia wanted? Did she think it was still her job to kill babies? Or to make me kill babies for her? Mostly, she just seemed full of anger. Like she wanted to hurt someone and anyone would do.

I could understand that.

"Leave me alone!" I shouted. "Just leave me alone!"

Grace rounded on me. "If you don't shut the hell up right now, I'm going to make you."

"If you don't shut the hell up, I'm going to make you."

A woman's hand over my mouth and nose, stopping me breathing. The smell of her sweaty fingers and the metal taste of rage in my mouth. I bite on to her palm. She swears and picks me up so my feet kick in the air. Somewhere there's a baby crying. Somehow the crying is my fault.

"I'll make you pay for that, you little monster."

"I'll make you pay for that," I yelled. I launched myself

on to Maisy, still cradled in Grace's arms. If I could shut
Maisy up, the woman in my head would go away. If Maisy
stopped crying, old Amelia wouldn't bother me any more.
I grabbed the nearest bit of Maisy I could reach – her leg.
Grace pulled back.

"What the hell do you think you're doing? Get away
from her!"

Jim came into the room. He looked at us – Grace with
her arms around Maisy, screaming at me, me pummelling
them with my clenched fists. He grabbed me and dragged
me away.

"Olivia, calm down. Calm down."

I could hear the panic in his voice. *He's scared of me.*

Grace and Maisy went out of the door. Jim put me
down. He sat on the chair by the fire, watching as I kicked
and raged.

"I hate you, I hate you. I wish you were dead. I wish
you were *dead*."

Sometimes, when I threw fits, I did it to annoy my
foster parents. Sometimes I did it because I was so angry
I had to let the anger out or explode. But now I did it
because it was either that or listen to my thoughts.

*He won't let you stay here now you've tried to hurt the
baby. You'll have to go.*

Afterwards, he tried to talk to me.

"You know that must never happen again?" he said.
"Olivia?"

There's a ghost in this house and she's trying to kill Maisy.

"I didn't do anything."

"Olivia. I'm serious. Maisy is only little. You *mustn't* try and hurt her."

I think I'm going mad.

"Or what? If I smack her in the nose, what will you do?"

Jim looked at me steadily.

He'll send you away. He'll send you away.

"You can't hurt a baby, Olivia. It's against the law, for one thing."

"Would you call the police, then?"

"I wouldn't let it get to that stage," said Jim. "If I honestly thought you were going to hurt Maisy, I'd have to make sure you weren't in a position to do so. I'd have no choice."

He doesn't love you. He doesn't even like you. He likes Maisy more than you, and Maisy can't even talk.

"Would you chuck me out?" I said. "Mr For Ever And Ever? Would you?"

"If I had to," said Jim. "Then, yes. I would."

WOULD YOU?

"Would you chuck me out? Mr For Ever And Ever? Would you?"

"If I had to," said Jim. "Then, yes. I would."

When I lived with my mum, I could always tell when she was going to hit me. When she'd had a bad day, when she'd run out of money, when she'd had just the right amount to drink – enough to make her angry, but not enough to make her fall asleep. I used to watch the anger building and building. The waiting would get so bad that I'd try and hurry it along. I'd ask annoying questions, or sing, or look happy, or sad, or do bouncing on the mattress when I'd been told not to. Anything, so the getting-hit would happen and I could stop worrying about it.

"Would you chuck me out? Mr For Ever And Ever? Would you?"

164

"If I had to. Then, yes. I would."

Waiting for Jim to chuck me out was like that. I could feel it *looming* like a monster waiting to pounce. *It's not safe to keep Olivia in a house with a cat. It's not safe to keep Olivia in a house with a little girl like Harriet. It's not safe to keep Olivia in a house with a baby.* I'd heard the same words, or words like them, said by all sorts of people who thought they loved me. They were probably true.

So if Jim was going to chuck me out, why didn't he just do it already?

"If you're going to chuck me out, why don't you do it already?" I said to Jim at breakfast.

"Who says I'm going to chuck you out?" said Jim.

"You are," I told him. "You *are*." And I threw my bowl of Coco Pops at his face.

I expected him to get angry. I *wanted* him to get angry. But he just carried on eating his porridge with milk dripping down his cheeks and into his beard.

"You look stupid," I told him. "You *are* stupid."

"That must be hard," said Jim. "Living with someone you think is stupid."

"*Yeah*," I said. "It *is*. You're stupid and pathetic and *horrible*, and I wish I lived with Liz instead of you."

"I'm sorry to hear that," said Jim, calmly. He didn't even *care*.

I picked up the milk bottle from the table and threw it at him, as hard as I could. I hoped it might break, but it didn't. It bounced off his face and rolled across the floor, spreading milk in a white puddle. Harriet squealed, and Grace said, "Olivia!" I stared at the puddle with a mixture of glee and horror. What was going to happen now?

"What the hell do you think you're doing?" said Grace. "Are you *insane*?"

"All right," said Jim. He stood up. "Come on, kids, let's let Olivia be. Harriet, bring your Coco Pops upstairs if you haven't finished them."

They all stood up and went upstairs. I followed.

"You're such a loser, I said. "I hate you. I *hate* you!"

They went into Jim's room and shut the door. I tried banging on it, but he wouldn't let me in.

"Why don't you just send me back to Fairfields?" I yelled. "I wish you would!"

And then I went downstairs and poured the contents of the teapot into Jim's coat pockets, just to make myself feel better.

Somewhere close by, a baby began to cry. It wasn't Maisy, because Maisy was still in Jim's room with Grace.

"Go to sleep, my baby, close your pretty eyes. . ."

"Shut up!" I yelled. "Stupid ghost baby!"

"Angels up above you are peeking through the skies. . ."

I could *feel* Amelia in the kitchen beside me. I could *feel* her anger. It tasted sharp and metallic in my mouth, like blood. It pounded like blood in my ears.

In the bedroom upstairs, Maisy started wailing.

"Make her stop!" I yelled. I ran upstairs and started kicking the bedroom door, like they do in films.

166

Maisy's wails increased. I wanted to smash her stupid face into the wall. Would that do it? Would Amelia leave me alone if I shut Maisy up for ever? The thought excited me and terrified me at the same time. I really would be a monster. Everyone would know how awful I really was. No one would ever dare try and love me again.

"Leave me alone!" I yelled. "Why don't you ever just leave me alone?"

"Great big moon is shining," Amelia was singing in my head. *"Stars begin to peep. It's time for little babies to go to sleep."*

BLOOD MAGIC

I went into my room. I pulled open the drawer of my bedside cabinet, unzipped my pencil case and took out the knife, the one I'd stolen from school. I tested its edge with the tip of my finger, and the blade cut through the skin. Blood pooled on my fingertip: deep, dark, thick and red. Like a magic potion. Like a magic spell. Like witchcraft.

Still sharp.

I think I might be a witch.

The knife didn't have a sheath, so I made one for it out of a cereal box and Sellotape, the way the big girls used to at Fairfields. Then I put the knife into the pocket of my red cardigan that Liz bought me, and buttoned up the pocket so nobody would know it was there. Liz's cardigan was big and old and woolly, and had been washed so many times it had pockets as big as the Doctor's in *Doctor Who*. Nobody could see the knife from the outside, but I knew it was there.

It made me feel safe, knowing my knife was nearby.

If I needed it, I'd be ready.

HOME NUMBER 7

JACKIE

I was five when Hayley and Jamie and I were taken into care for good. My mum had gone off, the way she did sometimes, only this time she hadn't come back. We'd been on our own for four days. We'd eaten all the cereal, and Jamie had drunk all his milk, and now he was crying because he was hungry and I couldn't make him stop. I was terrified that my mum really had forgotten us this time and was never coming back, but I didn't know how to get out of the flat. The door was a big metal one with no windows, and Mum had locked us in and taken the key. I could have shouted for help, I suppose, but I was worried about what Mum would do to me if she came back and found out what I'd done.

It was afternoon on the fourth day when someone started banging on the door. Hayley and I ran into Mum's room and hid under the bed, but Jamie started crying, so they knew we were in there.

"Open up!" a man shouted. "It's the police!" Then I knew they weren't going to go away, so I shouted through the door that we didn't have a key and they went quiet.

I don't remember how they got the door open, but I do remember them coming in in big fluorescent jackets, and talking on their walkie-talkies, and looking round our dirty, half-empty flat and shaking their heads. Mum sold the furniture when she ran out of money, which was often. Then they took us to a police station. Someone took Jamie away, but Hayley and I had to wait for hours and hours and hours, in the corner of this big office. I thought we were going to prison, because Mum always said I'd go to prison if I carried on being so bad.

Eventually, a new lady came and told us she was going to find us a nice home to stay in. I said I wanted my mum, and she told me Mum wasn't very well and couldn't look after us right now. I only found out years and years later that she was in prison. She hadn't even bothered to tell the police about us being locked in the flat. They only found out because we were on her file, and one of the policemen asked where we were.

The lady took Hayley and me in a car to a flat with a big fat lady called Jackie. I said, "We're supposed to be with our brother," and the lady said Jamie was staying in a different home, and we'd see him soon, but I never saw him again.

I said, "We want our mum."

And Jackie said, "You'll see your mum soon, pet," but we didn't. We didn't see her again for weeks and weeks, and then it was only for about an hour.

Jackie gave us a bath, and made us stand in the cold while she wrote down all the marks and bruises we had. It took for ever. Then she gave us some soup, which was brown and had horrible slimy bits of spaghetti floating in it. I hadn't eaten in over a day, but I felt more sick than hungry. The soup tasted gross, but I was scared to say so in case she hit me.

Afterwards, she made us go to bed in big T-shirts that had belonged to other kids before us, and were all thin and faded with too much washing. They made me even more frightened, because if she stole things off other kids, maybe she would steal our clothes too and we'd never get them back.

I didn't want to sleep in a bed on my own, so after she'd gone, I crept in with Hayley.

"Do you think we'll ever see Mum and Jamie again?" Hayley whispered.

"Course we will," I said.

"Are we living with this lady now?" said Hayley.

"Yes," I said, but I was wrong. Jackie was only an emergency foster carer. We stayed with her for a few days, until another social worker came along and said we were going to live with Donna and Craig now. Just until we went back to our mum.

SNAP

Something changed.

I stopped trying to be friends with Daniel and Harriet. I stopped trying to be nice to Liz. I stopped caring about what Grace said to me, and I stopped worrying about whether Jim liked me or not. I didn't care about any of that any more.

I snapped at Harriet when she asked me if I wanted to play dressing-up. I shouted at Daniel when he asked me if I wanted to go out on my bike. I screamed at Grace when she had a go at me for snapping and shouting and screaming. And Jim. . .

I was horrible to Jim. Totally, definitely, absolutely, utterly, completely horrible. I knew I was, the whole time I was being horrible, but I didn't stop. I spat at him. I threw things in his face. I kicked and screamed and bit

173

when he tried to get me to go into the dining room, or sit down and put my seatbelt on, or do whatever it was he wanted me to do today.

"I *hate* you!" I said to him, over and over and over again. "I *hate* you!"

I watched Daniel and Harriet moving further and further away from me. I watched them tense whenever I came through the door. I heard them talking about me in rooms where I wasn't. I could *feel* them whispering in the spaces I left behind. It was terrifying, how easy it was to push them away.

Jim fought, but he couldn't win, and he knew it. I could see it in the way he looked at me, the way his back clenched when I glared at him, the way his eyes flickered towards Harriet when I came into the room. I could see it in the slump of his shoulders when he told me to go into the dining room and I just laughed at him.

I was more powerful than thunder.

Jim tried to talk to me about it.

"Olivia, where did all this anger come from? What's happened?"

I wouldn't answer.

Daniel tried to talk to me too.

"Olivia, you know Amelia's ghost isn't real, don't you? It's just the man who runs the pub teasing Harriet."

"Teasing!" I said. "Murder and people killing themselves, teasing!"

"Well, stories, then. There isn't really a ghost here. I don't know why you hear things that aren't there, but I don't think it's Amelia Dyer. Maybe it's just . . . memories. Bad memories that won't be forgotten."

But isn't that what a ghost is?

Liz talked to me on Saturday, in Pizza Hut, after the football.

"I wonder if you're acting like this because you're worried Jim's going to ask you to leave," she said. Wondering Aloud was another Liz thing. Jim did it too, but only when he remembered.

"I don't care if he does ask me to leave," I said. "I don't like him anyway."

"He likes you," said Liz.

"No, he doesn't."

"Why doesn't he?"

This was why I hated Liz sometimes.

"*Because*," I said. "Can I have potato skins?"

"Because what?" said Liz, ignoring me. I don't know why she kept going on at me for being rude. She was nearly as bad.

"Because!" I shouted. I didn't mean to shout. It came out louder than I'd expected. "You know why. Because I'm evil."

"Olivia," said Liz, and I suddenly wanted to get out of there as fast as possible. "You aren't evil. You're *hurt*. Lots of bad things happened to you, and because of that you need to do things to make yourself feel safe, and that's OK, Olivia. That's what people who are hurt *do*."

Liz had said things like this lots of times before, but I never believed her.

175

"If it's OK," I said, "then why did you always punish me for doing it? Why do you keep telling me I have to be different for Jim, if it's not bad?"

Liz laughed. "That's a good question," she said. "It's because you might not be in control of your feelings, but you *are* in control of what you do with those feelings. All those tools we talked about – remember? I think life would be easier for you if you used them when you felt angry or scared, rather than just flipping out. I think you'd feel safer."

Huh. Helen kept going on about tools too. Stupid things like *use your words* and *count to ten*. They worked all right when I lived with Liz, but when I lived with Jim I was too frightened to remember them most of the time. When you're frightened, you don't have time to think *Is Daniel really saying he hates me, or does he just want to read his book?* You think *Daniel hates me!* and then you panic.

"So if I don't use my tools, am I bad?" I said.

"No," said Liz. "You're just scared. Everyone gets scared. When you're scared you make mistakes. And what I try to do is to help you find better ways of dealing with that."

"I don't make mistakes!" I said, furiously. I hated the smug way she said that, like I was just some stupid kid getting things wrong. "I do bad things *on purpose*. Because I *want to*."

"Well, then you're someone who does bad things," said Liz. "That doesn't make you a bad person. Actions are bad, but people are always more complicated."

Sometimes Liz just talked *nonsense*. I *hated* it, because I wanted her to protect me, and how could she do that when she was so wrong?

"There *are* bad people," I said. "There *are*. *Evil* people. Amelia's evil. Violet's evil. So's—" I stopped. I wasn't sure if my mum was evil or not. I *loved* my mum. "*I'm* evil," I said instead.

"Well, I know that's not true," said Liz. She ruffled my hair. I pulled away.

"Listen," she said. "Violet did some evil things. Things which should never have happened to you. But . . . she's not the things she did. She's a human being. Maybe she was ill. Maybe she was hurt herself. Look, I know you don't want to hear this, but it's important that you try. Jim likes you. He wants you in his family. And Daniel and Harriet like you too, and they want you to be their sister. I know it's hard for you to believe, but it's true. But, Olivia, Jim can't keep you in his house if it's not safe for Harriet and Maisy. That doesn't mean you're a bad person. It means Jim has to look out for all the kids in his house. OK?"

"But it's not *me*," I wailed. "It's Amelia."

She's trying to make me hurt Maisy. I don't want to, but I don't know how else to get her to leave me alone.

I wanted to say the words, but I couldn't. They really would chuck me out if I said that.

Liz waited. Then, when she could see I wasn't going to say anything else, she sighed. It was an Olivia's-being-stupid-and-annoying sigh.

"Look," she said. "Let's not fight. I love you. And I think you're a wonderful girl, and I'm sorry you're finding things so hard right now."

I hated it when people gave me stupid lying compliments like that. *Hi, Olivia, just wanted to tell you that the guy who's supposed to be your dad thinks you're so evil he doesn't want you in the same house as his family. But don't forget what a great kid you are!* And I hated, hated, hated that Liz was doing it worst of anybody, because now she was lying to me like everybody else.

"Shut up!" I shouted. "Shut up, shut up!" And I tipped the table up and over, spilling everything on to the floor with a *clatter, clash, shatter, crash, smash*.

SOMETHING TO HURT

When I first came to live with Jim, I hated my bedroom. But somehow – over the six months I'd lived there – it had become a place that belonged to me. The bed had my old red-and-blue-striped duvet cover from Liz's on it, and a hollow at the end where Zig-Zag liked to sleep in the afternoons. The bare notice board had gradually been filled up. There was a photo of me and Liz by a canal, another photo of me and Daniel and Harriet in our wedding clothes, eating wedding cake, and a picture of Hayley that Jim had found and stuck up when he finally unpacked my bags. Other things had found their way up there too: a postcard from Liz on holiday on the Isle of Man, one of Daniel's drawings of me as Wolverine, two Harriet drawings of us as zombies, and loads of stuff Harriet had presented me with over the last half year –

a lanyard, two friendship bracelets, and a flower and a monkey made out of Hama beads. There was a real sheep's skull that Daniel and I had found in a field, and a pile of stones and pine cones on the windowsill which I certainly wouldn't be allowed to take with me when I left.

There were big things too; things that had drifted in from the rest of the house, like Daniel's rounders bat and a rug Jim had let me take from one of the empty bedrooms. There was the big Dalek poster Liz gave me, and the stack of books we'd been reading, piled up on the bedside table. There was even an Asterix poster Jim had found rolled up in the attic and said I could have, though I wasn't sure if that was for always or just while I stayed here. Usually when I moved house, I had to leave things behind. Foster parents were forever chucking stuff out, or telling me to leave toys I'd grown out of for the other kids. If I was in charge, I'd never throw anything away, ever.

After I came home from seeing Liz, I sat on my bed and looked around my room. It made me edgy, how home-like it was starting to look. It made me afraid. It made me restless. I picked up the rounders bat and went into the corridor, looking for something to hurt.

"Olivia," Harriet said.

Harriet was standing in the doorway of her bedroom, watching me. Her dark little face was screwed up with something I couldn't read. Perfect Harriet. I wanted to smash her perfect little face in.

"Don't you want to be in our family any more?" she said.

I stared at her. *Don't you want to be in our family?* Of *course* I wanted to be in her family. Her family was brilliant. She was brilliant. I didn't just want her to be my sister, I wanted to *be* her. That's how brilliant she was.

"Your dad hates me," I said. "So I'm not in your family anyway."

Harriet chewed on her lip. "I thought you liked me," she said.

"Well, I *don't*," I said. "You're stupid and pathetic. I wish I'd never come here."

Harriet backed into her room.

"I thought you liked it here," she said.

"I *don't!*" I shouted, and I swung the bat at her – I stopped before the bat touched her arm, but only just.

Harriet flinched. I could see her tense. Her shoulders hunched, her head turned, her chin pressed itself down into her stomach to make herself as small as possible. She *cowered*.

"Stop it!" I shouted. "Stop looking like that!"

Harriet gave a little gasp. She didn't move. I took a step towards her.

"You're crazy," I told her. "I don't know why I ever wanted to be your sister. You're a boring, stupid, whiny, little crybaby."

I looked around the room for something to show how stupid she was.

"Look at this piece of crap," I said, and I dragged her doll's house out from beside the bed. I kicked it. A dent appeared in the wall.

Harriet made a strangled noise.

"Stop it!" she said. "Olivia! Stop it!"

I kicked the doll's house again. My shoe made a Godzilla-sized footprint on the wall. I swung the rounders bat with all my strength, straight into the doll's house roof.

Harriet screamed. She forgot she was scared of me and started tugging on my arm.

"Olivia! Stop it! Olivia!"

Smash. Smash. Smash.

Harriet started to cry.

"Daddy! *Daddy!*"

Thud. Smash.

Jim came into the room behind me and lifted me up and away. I kicked and howled, and swung the rounders bat back, trying to connect with his legs. Harriet was shrieking. Daniel was standing in the doorway. He looked appalled.

"Daddy!" screamed Harriet, but it was too late. The doll's house lay on its side, a rounders-bat hole in the roof.

They'll have to get rid of me now.

THE ONLY QUIET BABY IS A DEAD BABY

Jim didn't know what to do. Harriet was sobbing like I'd just eaten her kitten. I stopped struggling, and he relaxed his grip a little. I waited to see what would happen next. What would Jim do? *I don't care what he does*, I thought, but I did. Of course I did.

"Olivia—" Jim said, but Harriet grabbed his arm and sobbed, "Daddy—" and he turned back to comfort her.

I charged forward, out of his arms, threw the rounders bat on to the floor and ran down the stairs. Jim let me go. I ran through the kitchen and into the yard. I didn't want to listen to him lecturing me about how he had to keep Harriet safe. What about keeping me safe?

"You know we still love you, sweetheart. You'll always be our little girl, whatever happens."

That's what Dopey Graham said when he dumped

me. Dopey Graham. I saw him maybe twice after that, I think. I scratched *YOU WILL DIE* into the side of his car with his car key, and he never came back.

"I think you scared him off," said my social worker, when I asked her when he was coming. I was nine. I was pretty horrible to him, but he still should have come back more than twice.

I wondered if Jim would say something like that when he dumped me. I didn't *think* he would, but if he did, I thought I really might kill him. I could do it, I bet. I put my hand on the knife, still there in my cardigan pocket. They wouldn't be able to send me to someone like Violet if I killed Jim. They'd have to put me in prison. Violet couldn't get me in prison, and I bet no one else would either. I'd be the eleven-year-old murderer, and no one would dare do anything to me in case I killed them too. And I *would* kill them. I'd strangle them like old Amelia used to. I'd strangle them all.

But would Amelia follow me to prison?

The farmyard was empty and boring. I wandered out into the garden. The patio at the back of the house was thick with weeds – evil-looking nettles and thistles and sticky burrs. I walked straight through them, not caring when the nettles slapped against my bare legs. They couldn't hurt me. Nothing could hurt me, because I didn't care. I didn't care if Jim dumped me. I didn't care if they made me go and live with Violet, or someone even worse.

The grass on the lawn was up to my thighs. I waded through it. Once upon a time, this garden must have been beautiful. Was it beautiful when old Amelia lived here? I came to the end of the lawn and out into the flower beds at the other side, the ones where Harriet thought Amelia's babies were buried. I bet she was right. I bet there were dead babies there. Those flower beds always gave me the creeps. It smelled different here; wet and mouldy and rotten. Bushes grew out of the earth, clogged with nettles and dandelions and weeds.

I crouched down and dug my hand into the soil, enjoying the wet mud against my fingers. Jim would want me to wash them, but I wouldn't. I wouldn't do anything anyone told me to, ever again.

Amelia was there.

I could smell her. Tobacco and alcohol and milk and old, dry skin. And a sense of evil. Of *hatred*. I remembered: this was where she'd found me, that first day when Daniel and I fought and I ran into the garden. If the babies really were buried here, this was where Amelia would be strongest. This was where she'd be able to hurt me most.

It was a dark day. It was supposed to be summer, but the sky was grey, and the sun was hiding behind the clouds. I clenched my fists in the earth, waiting.

I heard a noise. A woman, laughing. I looked over my shoulder. Nothing. Then the same laughter, from the other side of the garden. I scrambled to my feet and backed away, keeping my eyes fixed on the place where the noise was coming from. The laughter again, this time from behind me. I spun round. Nothing.

185

I could never escape her. Never. Wherever I went, she'd be there.

I clenched my fingers tight. "Go away," I said, out loud. "Please. Leave me alone."

Laughter again, closer. I closed my eyes, and then opened them quickly, because not knowing what was coming was worse. And then I felt it. A hand, touching my neck. Cold, dry skin against mine. I could feel the calluses under her fingertips. I could feel the rough fabric of her skirts, brushing against my back. Her hand on my neck. The world swayed, blurring in and out of focus.

"Leave me alone," I said again. I thought she wasn't going to answer, and then I heard her. Amelia Dyer, or was it Violet? Or my mum? I couldn't tell the difference any more. It was simply someone who hated me.

Laughing.

The front door was still open. I tried to sneak back into the house without Jim noticing, but he was in the kitchen, on his laptop. He stuck out his hand as I went past.

"Olivia."

"Let me go!"

"Olivia, calm down."

"I *am* calm! You're the one making me not be calm!"

"It's going to take a long time to fix Harriet's doll's house," said Jim. "So you owe me—"

"I don't owe you anything!" I shouted. "You owe me! You owe me all the toys Daniel and Harriet have! You owe me a bike, and a skateboard, and karate lessons, and all those books in Daniel's bookcase, and—"

"It must be hard—" Jim said, but I shoved him. I didn't want him to be sensible and sympathetic. I wanted him to punish me.

"Olivia, you need to go to the dining room now," Jim said, very quietly.

I opened my mouth to say no and suddenly I was back at Liz's house, the day she threw me out.

"I'll kill you!" I say, and I punch her as hard as I can in the stomach.

"Olivia, go to your room," says Liz, but,

"I won't!" I say, and I punch her again.

"Olivia?" said Jim.

I couldn't bear it.

I backed away and ran out of the kitchen, down the dark little passage into the living room. The walls pushed against me. I'd been locked in the dark. Everyone was happier when I wasn't there. I could hear my mum singing, and Hayley laughing, and everyone having a good time without me.

"Let me out!" I shout, but someone's covered my mouth with parcel tape, and nothing comes out. I try to wriggle, but someone's taped up my arms, and I can't breathe, and. . .

"You belong to me," says old Amelia.

I crammed my hands over my ears and banged through into the living room. Grace was sitting by the fire making a house out of university prospectuses for Maisy. She looked up when I came in and scowled at me.

187

"Hello," she said, in a hello-you-little-toerag voice.

"Shut up!" I yelled. "Don't say anything! Shut up!"

"Look," said Grace. "I've had enough of this. I don't care what happened to you. You can't just—"

"Leave me *alone!*" I screamed, and Maisy started to wail.

"Now look what you've done!" said Grace. She picked Maisy up and started joggling her. I crammed my fingers into my ears and buried my head under the sofa cushion, but I could still hear the screaming.

"Now look what you've done, you little monster."

I'm in a room, a dark room with no carpet and chunks missing from the walls. It might be one of the flats we lived in with Mum, I'm not sure. It's cold and damp, and smells of something rotting. I'm on the floor. Somewhere, a baby is crying.

I was back in the living room. Maisy was howling. Grace was walking around the room, holding her, saying, "Shh, shh."

"Make her *stop!*" I yelled.

Grace rounded on me. "This is your fault, you idiot. Be quiet!"

"This is your fault," says someone. Someone is a tall, dark shadow against the wall, with meaty hands and a black bonnet. Someone smells of tobacco and sweat and fury. "If you don't make that kid shut up, I'm going to drop you over a bleeding railway bridge."

Maisy's howls were growing louder. Grace was muttering to herself as she rocked her. My mum used to mutter just like that. It meant something bad was going to happen, probably to me. I stuck my hand in my cardigan pocket and found my knife. I eased it out of its cardboard sheath, and gripped the handle.

A way out.

The room smells of coal and burnt wood and something wet and rotting.

"If you don't make that kid shut up," says Amelia, clear in my head. "I'm going to drop you over a bleeding railway bridge."

I leapt.

BLOOD AND THUNDER

There was blood everywhere.

There was blood all over my red cardigan that Liz gave me, and blood all down Grace's back. Grace was yelling at me. Maisy was screaming.

I don't know why. I hadn't hurt her at all. I hadn't even scratched her. I *meant* to, but Grace got in the way.

Then Jim's arms were around me, pulling me away. I fought and kicked and howled, while Maisy screamed, and my knife was sticky with blood, and Harriet stood in the doorway and cried and cried.

Jim lifted me up and carried me into the yard. Then he locked the front door. I hammered on it with my fists. Then I kicked it. *Thud. Thud. Thud.* It rattled in the hinges, and I wondered if I could kick it down. I could smash the kitchen window in, but once I thought that, I knew I didn't want to go inside. I was too worried about what I might see.

He was going to throw me out. What choice did he have? I'd stabbed Grace. I'd tried to kill Maisy. I could feel the panic fluttering in my stomach. Who would they send me to next? Another Violet. A children's home with big kids who would beat me up. Prison.

Thud. Thud. Thud.

There was blood everywhere.

I was an attempted murderer. What was going to happen to me now?

Jim's friend Alison arrived, and Jim and Grace went off to the hospital with Maisy. I got scared when I saw them coming, and went and hid behind the barn door. Grace was covered in blood. So was Jim. But Grace was walking out to the car, so I figured she couldn't be too hurt. And Maisy had stopped crying. Jim was holding her under one arm, and his other arm was around Grace.

He didn't look round to see if I was there. It was like he'd wiped me out of his head, the way my mum, and Mummy and Daddy, and Annabel and Graham did when I left. This morning he was supposed to be my dad, and now I wasn't even worth a glance.

I went down to the garden with the fountain and the flower beds and Amelia's ghost. I waited for someone to come and find me, but nobody did. I kept expecting the police to turn up and haul me away, like they did that time I punched Liz in the stomach, but they didn't. I crouched down in the weeds and hugged my knees.

Nobody came.

I wished I was dead.

After what felt like for ever, Daniel came down the garden path. I sat there with my arms around my legs watching him. I could see Alison's face looking out of the window, watching me. I stuck my finger up at her, but she didn't look away.

"Hello," he said uncertainly.

"I wouldn't get too close," I told him. "I might kill you too."

"No, you won't," said Daniel. He crouched down beside me and picked up a handful of gravel. He tossed it from hand to hand, thoughtfully. "Dad phoned," he said. "Grace needed six stitches."

That sounded like a lot.

"Does she hate me?" I said.

"I don't know," said Daniel. "They're coming home, Dad said. Are you OK?"

"Of course I'm OK," I said. "Why wouldn't I be? It wasn't me! It was Amelia!"

"It looked like you," said Daniel.

"Well, it wasn't."

It was. Of course it was.

Daniel let the gravel trickle out of his hands. "Don't you care about Grace at all?" he asked.

I didn't know what to say. Of course I cared. There just wasn't enough space in my head to care about me and

Grace and Amelia all at the same time.

"What's your dad going to do to me?" I whispered.

"I don't know," said Daniel.

It was late when Jim got home. We were supposed to be in bed, but I had my light on and horrible Alison hadn't told me to switch it off. Probably she was scared of me. She hadn't shouted at me about Grace. Nobody had. Somehow that made everything worse. It was like everyone was afraid to talk to me, in case I stabbed them too.

I lay awake and listened to Jim and Alison talking in low voices. At last I heard the *clunk* of the front door shutting and Jim's footsteps on the stairs. I waited for him to come into my room, but he didn't. I heard his footsteps in the bathroom, the sound of water running. Surely he wasn't going to ignore me? He must be able to see my light.

The footsteps came down the hall. They stopped outside my room. I waited. The door opened, and Jim's head appeared.

"Turn that light off, Olivia," he said. "It's time you were asleep."

"I can't sleep," I said. "Read to me!"

"Not tonight," said Jim. "Come on, now."

"What's going to happen?" I said. I didn't mean to ask, but it just came out without my planning it.

Jim hesitated.

"Let's talk about this in the morning, shall we?" he said. "Get some sleep."

"No!" I was properly frightened now. "Tell me. Are you going to chuck me out?"

Jim didn't answer.

"You are!" I said. "Aren't you?"

"I'm sorry, Olivia," Jim said. "I can't let something like this happen again."

"Where are they going to send me?" I whispered.

"I don't know," said Jim.

It was honest, at least. If he'd said *Everything's going to be all right*, I think I really might have killed him.

CATHY AND BILL

Hayley and Jamie and I lived with my mum until I was five, but lots of times before that we got sent to live with other people for a little bit, when she was drinking too much and couldn't look after us.

I don't remember exactly how many families we lived with before we got taken into care for good. Liz looked it up for me once and said there were five, but I can only remember three. There was an old lady with a house full of old things – china ladies, and leather books, and cups and plates all different colours, and a piano that she used to let Hayley and me make up tunes on.

There were two ladies who lived together and took foster kids too small to go to school. The house was always noisy, and there were always loads of toys everywhere. They were always shouting:

"Stop hitting your sister!"

"Leave that alone!"

"What did I say? Did I say no? Did I?"

The family I remember best was the one we went to just after Jamie was born. They were a mum and a dad, and they lived in a little village, which I remember as being sunny all the time. They didn't have many toys, but it didn't matter because they had this enormous garden with a climbing frame, and a tyre swing, and trees to climb in, and a big patio that they used to let us draw on with chalks, and two cats who used to climb into my bed at night and keep me safe.

The mum's name was Cathy and the dad's name was Bill. They used to call Hayley "Sweetiepie" and me "Trouble", but in a nice way, like they didn't mind me being naughty and thought it was kind of funny.

"What's up, Trouble?" Bill used to say, and I'd tell him all the things I was going to do that day. If they were things he didn't want me to do, like climbing on the roof or eating all the ice cream, he'd say, "I wouldn't do that if I were you, Trouble. I might get hungry and gobble you up!" And he'd make biting noises and pretend to eat me up. At first I thought he was serious, but when I realized he was only playing, he used to make me giggle all over.

Bill had a big bike with a child seat on the back of it, and when he cycled anywhere he used to strap me into the seat and take me with him. I'd sit there with the wind blowing through my hair and my bare legs dangling down on either side, and I'd pretend that Bill was my daddy and we were going to live there for ever. When I got angry, he used to hold me – firmly, but not too tight. I usually hate it when people hold me, but with Bill I didn't mind. Perhaps because I was so little and he was so gentle. Sometimes when I get angry, it's terrifying, because it's so big and so horrible; because I stop being Olivia and turn into some sort of monster, and I don't know what the monster wants to do or who it's going to hurt. But in Cathy and Bill's house, the monster was never bigger than Bill's arms.

I don't remember much else about them. They had a bonfire once, and we toasted marshmallows. They used to read us stories at bedtime. Jamie never cried on and on and on, like he did at home.

When my social worker said we had to go back to live with my mum, I remember Cathy getting very upset. She cried, and argued, and on the day she had to give us back, she held me very tight and said, "I wish I could keep you," and I didn't know what to feel, because I loved it at Cathy and Bill's house, but I loved my mum too.

Cathy and Bill were probably the last people who ever wanted me. If we'd been allowed to stay, I bet they'd have adopted us. They've probably adopted some other kids since then, and they wouldn't want me now anyway. Mums and dads only want you when you're little and sweet. Eleven is much too old to be adopted again.

GHOSTS

The Iveys chucked me out, of course.

Home number seventeen was these two men called Andy and Chris. They were all right. They lived in a little house on the edge of Bristol. My room was small and plain, with some other kid's chewing gum stuck to the bottom of the bed.

The first night I was there, Liz rang.

"Don't start, all right!" I shouted at her.

"Olivia," she said. "Calm down. I didn't say anything."

"It wasn't my fault!" I shouted. "I didn't do it! He just chucked me out for no reason!"

"Olivia—" said Liz.

"I didn't!" I shouted. "Don't shout at me! She made me do it!"

"I'm not shouting at you," said Liz. "Who made you do it? Amelia Dyer?"

"Oh, forget it," I said, and banged the phone down, hard. I thought she would probably ring back, but she didn't.

Liz wasn't the only person who wanted to talk about what had happened. Loads of people were talking about me, all the time, with or without me there. I heard Andy talking to Liz on the phone, and Chris talking to Carole, late at night when they thought I was in bed. Carole wanted me to go back to Fairfields. Liz thought I should be in a family, but maybe not one with other children in it. I wondered what Andy and Chris thought, hearing all this stuff about how dangerous I was.

It felt weird living in a house with no other kids. At Jim's, there was always someone to play with and something going on somewhere. Here, there was nothing. When Andy and Chris were at work I had to go to a stupid play scheme, where all the other kids knew each other already and there were crazy rules about stuff like how long you were allowed to go on the trampoline, which they knew and I didn't, so I kept getting told off. I hated it. But when I got home it was even worse. I was allowed to play on Andy's DS for half an hour every day, and watch TV for another half an hour. I was allowed to ride my bike in the street, but no further than the end of the road, and it wasn't like there were any other kids to play with anyway, so mostly I didn't. Sometimes Andy and Chris played board games with me, but mostly I was stuck on my own. I hadn't lived without other kids since I lived with Liz, and I'd forgotten how lonely it was.

The only good thing about Andy and Chris's house was that Amelia wasn't there. But even that was sort of bad because I knew she was still at Jim's house, and I couldn't stop worrying about what she might be doing. Was she haunting Harriet now, instead of me? Or Grace? I thought she might be haunting Grace, because Grace was a bit like that other girl who had a baby without a husband. I was surprised by how much I minded about that. I didn't think it really mattered if I got sent to prison, because living in prison probably wouldn't be that different from living in Fairfields, but Grace was different. Grace was going off to university. I realized I didn't want anything bad to happen to Grace, and that surprised me. I never usually cared what happened to other people.

Life with Andy and Chris was OK. It wasn't *dreadful*. It was just . . . nothing. Empty, and flat, like a balloon after all the air has been burst out of it. A deflated balloon. That's what I felt like.

Even though Amelia wasn't at Andy and Chris's house, I still thought about her. I dreamed about her. In my dreams she was old and fat and evil. She sat by the coal fire in the living room and smoked her pipe and plotted her evil plots. Other times she sat in the garden, by the overgrown flower beds, wishing terrible things on Grace and Maisy and Jim and anyone who moved into that house for ever.

I hated that I'd done what she wanted me to. I hated that she'd taken the Iveys from me. It felt like she'd *won*. Losing to Amelia felt worse than losing to Daniel or Liz or someone I liked. Amelia winning felt like Violet winning, or the worst of the big girls at Fairfields, and I *hated* it. It made me want to fight. I was always fighting, against people who thought they could tell me what to do, against people who tried to make me feel small or ashamed, against people who thought they could make me care. But I'd never wanted to fight *for* something. It was a new feeling, and I wasn't sure if I liked it.

I asked Helen how you beat a ghost, but she thought I was asking how you beat a flashback, and kept going on about stupid tools and exercises and all that sort of thing.

"I don't mean stupid brain stuff!" I yelled at her. "I mean a ghost! I mean Amelia! A real, mad, evil, homicidal ghost!"

"Olivia. . ." Helen said, but I was too angry to listen.

"No!" I yelled. "Just give me something! *Anything!*"

"OK," said Helen. "Calm down. Olivia, calm down." I didn't want to calm down, but Helen just sat there waiting until I did.

"OK," said Helen. "Can you remember what I told you about fear and being frightened?"

I shook my head.

"Well," said Helen, "your brain is a machine for making connections. You're scared of the dark because your brain noticed that bad things happened to you in dark places – because of all the times your mother and Violet

201

punished you by locking you up. So the way to combat that is to teach your brain a new pattern – to show it that not all places in the dark are frightening. You do that by experiencing some dark places which aren't scary, and gradually your brain makes new connections. We haven't been doing that because it needs to happen at a pace you're comfortable with – and I think if I forced you to sit in dark rooms, it would probably be counter-productive, wouldn't it? But I think that's how I'd show Amelia that I wasn't scared of her. I'd think about the things that trigger her arrival; things like being on your own, babies, babies crying and night. And then I'd start repatterning your brain by exposing it to lots of unscary babies and nights, and that would teach it that those things were OK."

"And then Amelia would go away?"

"Yes. I think she would."

I thought that solution sounded a bit rubbish, personally. I was exposed to night *every single night* and it was still scary. And how was I supposed to be exposed to babies when Grace hated me now and was never going to let me near Maisy again?

But I liked what she said about showing Amelia I wasn't scared of her. I could see that that might work. I thought perhaps Amelia might be a bit like kids who try and pick on you at school. If you're scared of them, they win. But if you smash their faces in, they leave you alone.

I am an expert at face-smashing. I am an expert in bringing down grown-ups too. You just have to find their weak spot, and then you push it and push it and push it until they collapse into a little heap on the floor. I didn't think Amelia was the collapsing sort, but I knew where her weak spot was all right. It was the patch of garden by the fountain, the dark, evil, weedy bit at the end of the lawn. Whenever I went down there, Amelia always went after me. Grumpy Annabel used to get angry in just the same way whenever I started mocking her about what a crap mother she was. My mum always went after me if I looked happy when she was in a crap mood. I'd never liked the end of the garden, but Amelia had really started going after me there after Harriet told me it was where she'd buried the babies. Perhaps, I thought, she really *had* buried them there.

I wondered what would happen if we found them.

I called Daniel on his mobile phone.

"Watch out," I told him. "I'm coming back!"

WHAT HARRIET FOUND

It was dead easy to get to Jim's house. The first thing I did was steal a purse from the bag of one of the play-scheme leaders. I picked the youngest and dopiest-looking one, and she didn't even tell anyone she'd lost it.

When Andy dropped me off at the play scheme the morning after that, I went in the door, hid in the loo until he'd gone, and then came out and went to the taxi line at the train station. Then I just got into a taxi and gave the driver Jim's address. I stuck close behind this other family in the queue, so it *sort of* looked like I was one of them, and they knew I was getting a taxi and were OK with it. The driver didn't say anything when I got in. Probably he thought a stupid farm in the middle of nowhere wasn't a very likely place to go and cause trouble.

Daniel and Harriet were waiting at the end of the

road, where I'd told them to be. I hadn't told them what I needed them to do, just that I was coming back.

"Stop!" I shouted at the taxi driver.

"Do your parents know you're here?" he said.

"That's none of your business!" I told him. "Stop asking stupid questions or I won't pay!"

"They know," said Daniel quickly. "She's my cousin. Olivia, give him the money and come on."

I counted out the money and climbed out of the taxi before the driver could say anything else. He muttered something and drove off.

Harriet ran over to me and put her arms around my waist. She squeezed so hard I thought I was going to choke.

"Hey! Let me breathe!"

"I missed you," said Harriet, but she let me go. I looked across at Daniel. He was frowning.

"Where did you get all that money?" he said.

"I stole it," I said. "Why? Are you going to tell the police?"

"No. . ." said Daniel, but he didn't look very happy. "Why do you always have to do such stupid things, Olivia?"

"How else was I supposed to get here? Oh, please, grumpy foster dad! Take me back to Daniel's house so I can murder his baby sister? Come on!"

I grabbed his hand and tried to pull him up the path, but he wouldn't come.

"Look," he said. "What *are* you doing here? Exactly?"

"I'm fighting Amelia," I said. My plan sounded a bit stupid now I had to explain it. "I'm showing her I'm not afraid of her any more. So I'm going to go where she's weakest, where she doesn't want me to go. And then – I dunno – find out why."

Daniel made a frustrated sort of noise. Harriet giggled.

"I know!" he said. "I know! Don't tell me! The flower beds, right? Amelia Dyer's hidden two hundred gold doubloons and the Thermos flask of eternal youth under the marigolds, and if we dig them up all Olivia's problems will go away and Dad will adopt her and we'll all live happily ever after? Right?"

He wasn't going to help. He was going to tell his dad on me, and Jim was going to send me back to Andy and Chris's, and Amelia was going to carry on haunting their house and making people kill babies for ever, and maybe she was going to go after Grace next, and there was nothing I could do about it.

I charged at Daniel and started kicking him. He stumbled back.

"Hey! Stop it!"

I grabbed his hair and yanked on it as hard as I could. Harriet hopped up and down, squealing, her voice getting higher and higher as she got more and more anxious.

"Olivia! Stop it!"

"It's not funny!" I snarled at Daniel. I yanked on his hair. I could smell his fear – sharp and close. Fear – someone else's fear – always makes me angry.

"OK! It's not funny! Jesus, Olivia, what was that for?"

"We *have* to find what she's hidden there," I said. "It's corpses, like Harriet said, I bet you anything. We *have* to find them. Otherwise it won't matter if Jim dumps me, *Maisy will be dead anyway*. Amelia will find some other way to kill her, I *know* she will."

I could tell he didn't believe me, but I didn't care. Just so long as he helped.

We tramped up the hill to the house. Daniel went to steal the shed key from Jim's office. For some reason he didn't let foster kids mess around with weedkiller, hedge trimmers and garden shears.

Can't imagine why.

Daniel and I took a spade each, and Harriet took a trowel. I led the way over to the flower bed. Even in the middle of the morning, it still felt creepy. It smelled of wet earth and mouldering leaves and tree bark and Amelia. I had that awful, skin-crawlingy feeling that someone was watching me, someone evil. I wanted to turn around and run away, but I remembered about Maisy and didn't.

"Here," I said. "I dunno. Somewhere here. Just dig."

So we dug.

At first, if I concentrated on digging and tried not to think about Amelia, it was almost fun. Like digging a hole at the seaside for the tide to fill. But pretty quickly it got boring. And then it got hard. The earth was full of all these little stones that you had to dig out with the corner of your spade. Sometimes you hit really big stones and then you had to stop and dig all the way around them to get them out, which usually meant making your hole twice as big. The further down you went, the harder it got, because your spade had less space to bend in.

We dug for ages. Much longer than I'd expected. Amelia didn't show up at all. The deeper we dug, the less I could feel her there. After a while, I stopped being able to smell her too.

If it had just been me, I'd probably have given up after about two minutes, but with Harriet and Daniel there, I couldn't. I could just imagine the look on Daniel's face if I gave in. And Harriet was pretty keen. Her job was the easiest because she had the trowel, so every time Daniel or I got stuck, we'd call her in and she'd start ferreting around under whatever big stone it was that was stuck, trying to lever it up. The sky was clear and white and still. Not exactly warm, but not freezing either. It smelled of earth and wet leaves and grass and no Amelia. It smelled good. I felt happier than I had in ages.

"Why would she put them so *deep*?" Harriet said.

"She probably didn't," said Daniel. "Just think of all the new soil getting made, piling on top of the old stuff."

I didn't know soil got made. I thought it just *was*, like mountains, or the pyramids.

Harriet was still digging away at her bit of rock.

"Can you help?" she said. "It goes down all that way."

I got out my spade and went over. "Where?" I said. "Here?" I smashed my spade down. The rock went *crunch*.

"You broke it!" said Harriet, accusingly.

"It's a rock!" I said. "Isn't it?"

I pressed down on the rock again with my spade. *Crunch*.

208

"That's not a rock," said Daniel. "That's a skull."

"What sort of skull?" said Harriet, anxiously. "Is it a dog?"

"I don't know," said Daniel. "Olivia, stop. You're crushing it. Be careful."

"It's not a dog skull," I said. "It's a human skull. It's one of Amelia's babies."

AMELIA AND THE DEAD BABY

Daniel and Harriet and I dug the soil out from all around the baby.

"We should tell the police," said Daniel.

"Why?" said Harriet.

"Well. It's a body. It's a crime scene."

"No, it's not," I said. "It's . . . archaeology."

"You don't know that," said Daniel. But I did.

"We should tell Dad," said Harriet, but, "Let's dig it out first," I said. Once Jim arrived there would be explanations and tellings-off and calling-Andy-and-Chrises and punishments, which wouldn't come from Jim because he wasn't my dad any more. I liked digging things with Daniel and Harriet. I wanted to pretend they were still my brother and sister for just a little bit longer.

The baby was a perfect skeleton, lying on its side in

the earth, still wrapped in the remains of a muddy grey blanket. Under the blanket, you could see raggedy bits of old clothes, half-rotted away and covered in earth.

"What do you think her name was?" said Harriet.

"Maybe she didn't have one," said Daniel. "Maybe she was just born."

"She was older than that," I said. "She's nearly as big as Maisy."

"We *should* tell Dad," said Daniel, and he stood up before I could argue.

"Me too!" said Harriet. "I want to tell him too!"

They ran off and left me there with the baby. I sat and looked at her. She was small and dead and not very human-looking.

As I sat there, I heard something in the trees. Something like a sigh, the sort of sigh you might make when you sat down at the end of a long walk, or laid something heavy to rest. The trees rustled, and then took up the noise, and for a moment it was as if the whole garden around me was sighing.

Or maybe it was just the wind.

I touched a piece of the baby's blanket, which was stiff with earth. The baby smelled of mud and wet leaves and something old and musty and sad. She didn't smell of Amelia. I couldn't smell Amelia anywhere – just the trees, and the flowers, and the wet-garden smell, and Andy and Chris's child shampoo.

She's gone, I thought. *Amelia's gone.* And I knew I ought to feel happy, but all I felt was quiet and sad and defeated.

They still don't want me, I thought. *Even if Amelia's gone, nobody wants me here.* And I just felt like crawling into the earth with the dead baby and never coming out again.

HOME NUMBER 1

MUM

I left my mum when I was five, but I can still remember loads about her. She was tall and skinny, and she had dark hair like me, only hers was longer and scragglier. She wore loads of rings and bracelets. She had a tattoo of a butterfly on her right arm.

Sometimes my mum was nice and sometimes she was horrible. When she was nice, she was lovely. She used to put on loud music and dance around the house, and we all had to dance with her. She'd sing, "Baby, can I hold you tonight?" and swing me up in the air. My best thing in the world was sitting in her lap while she plaited my hair, and told me stories about the beautiful house we were going to live in when she was rich, and all the toys she was going to buy us, and how happy we were going to be.

"How much do you love me?" she'd ask Hayley and

me, and we'd spread out our arms as wide as they'd go and say, *"This much!"*

I loved my mum so much, but she hated me. I was evil. I was a devil baby. She loved Hayley, and my baby brother Jamie. They were little and sweet and funny. I wasn't.

Other people's mums were lovely all the time. But other people's mums didn't have to look after me. I was so bad, it drove her crazy.

"You're so *stupid!*" my mum used to yell at me. "Why can't you just *die* and let me be happy?" She tried to beat the badness out of me, but it didn't go away. She used to hit me with an umbrella, or a shoe, or anything she could grab. I knew she was going to do it, but I was still bad. So it was my fault I got hit.

When my mum was done hitting me, she used to lock me in the cupboard and push the bed in front of the door, so I couldn't get out. It was very dark. Sometimes she left me there for hours and hours and hours. I could hear her singing, and Hayley and Jamie laughing. They always had lots of fun without me.

I knew I was five, because that's what Mum told the lady in the suit, who sniffed, and sometimes took us away to live in other houses. Five was quite big, but I never had a birthday party, or a cake, or presents. I asked my mum why once, and she said, "If you want a party, you'd better bloody behave yourself, hadn't you?"

I think probably my mum forgot when my birthday was. She was very forgetful. She forgot to buy food, and she forgot to change Jamie's nappy, and then shouted at him for crying.

"Shut the hell up screaming!" She used to get drunk and forget that I was in the cupboard, and sometimes she went away for days and days and locked us in the house and forgot all about us.

I had to look after Hayley and Jamie, but I wasn't very good at it. I couldn't stop Jamie crying, and I couldn't make food for us. Once, I cut my hand trying to open a can of beans and got blood all over the floor. I tried to wipe it up but it didn't work and my mum beat me with a leather belt when she came home. But usually there wasn't any food, and Hayley and Jamie would cry because they were hungry, and I didn't know what to do.

I always knew when my mum was going to hit me. I could see her getting angry, dropping things, going, "Crap, crap, crap, crap, crap, crap, crap."

Usually when she ran out of cider, I got hit.

The waiting was the worst part. When I knew it was going to happen, I always tried to hurry it up, so it was over.

These were the things I could do to make her hit me faster. I could:

Ask questions.

Whine. Like, "My *shoes* hurt," or "I'm *hungry*."

Crying was good too. So was looking sad, or looking happy, or making noise when she had a bad head.

"You're not my daughter."

That's what my mum said. Sometimes I thought she was right.

The things about me that were different from Hayley and Jamie were:

Hayley and Jamie were pretty and yellow-haired. I was skinny and dark-haired and ugly.

They made my mum smile. I made her angry.

I wasn't like the other children at the schools and nurseries our foster mothers took us to. I didn't know what to do with dolls or train sets. I didn't know how to listen to stories. The other kids played with each other, but they didn't play with me. I didn't understand their games, and I always got them wrong.

Sometimes I thought that I wasn't a real person. I was an alien, or a witch, or a monster in a human body. But deep down, I knew this wasn't true. I didn't look like Hayley and Jamie, but I did look like my mum. I expect when I grow up, I'll be just like her too.

I don't want to be like my mum, but I don't know how else to be.

BABIES IN THE FLOWER BED

It wasn't one of Amelia's babies who was buried in the flower bed. It was five.

"Five babies!" said Harriet. This was later. She and Jim came to Andy and Chris's house to see me. She was bouncing up and down with excitement. "Five babies in *our* garden. And we never knew!"

"*I* knew," I said.

"Olivia," said Jim. He knelt down beside me so his face was level with mine. "You didn't really know. Harriet and I both told you that was probably where Amelia would have buried her babies. It turns out we were right, that's all."

"But I could *feel* her!" I said.

"I know you thought you could feel her," he said. "But—"

I didn't want to hear any more. "You don't know what

217

you're talking about!" I said. "So just shut up!"

I expected Jim to get angry, but he just sighed. "You're probably right," he said. "Here. I'm sorry." He went to put his arm around my shoulder, but I pushed him away.

"Don't touch me!" I said. "Don't you even *touch* me!"

There was a proper police camp up at Jim's house. Policemen and Do-Not-Cross tape and dogs and all sorts of stuff. They stayed for days, until they'd found all the babies.

I didn't get to see most of it, because I was still living with Andy and Chris. I got to hear about it though, because Harriet kept ringing me up and giving me the latest body count.

"There's a reporter wants to talk to us!" she squeaked. "But Dad said no! And the police keep asking us questions."

"They think your dad did it," I told her. "Or me!"

The story was on the local news, and in the newspaper. It was totally unfair. The one time in my life I had the chance to be famous, and it was ruined by me living at the wrong house. If I'd still been living at Jim's, I bet I would have got on TV. *And* in the newspaper. Probably the story of my tragic life would have been written about in newspapers all across the country, and some rich family would have decided they wanted to adopt me. I never even got to see the crime scene, just pictures of it on the telly. I wanted to go and visit, but Andy and Chris said no.

The police talked to me too, the day after we found the bodies. A man and a woman.

"Tell me in your own words what happened," the woman said.

"Well," I said, "I knew there was something in the flower bed because Amelia kept going mental whenever I went near it."

"This is the baby farmer?"

"Yeah. Amelia Dyer. She's this woman who used to live in Jim's house in Victorian times. She murdered over four hundred babies, and then she was hanged for mass murder. She used to haunt the house, and make me try and kill Grace's baby. She's gone now, but probably not to heaven, because she was evil. Though Liz says people aren't evil, they just do evil things, so maybe she did."

"I see." The policewoman looked like she didn't really know what to say. "And . . . what do you mean by *going mental*?"

"Oh, you know. Screaming at me and telling me I was evil. Usual bad ghost stuff."

The police talked to me for ages, but it was a pretty stupid conversation. I thought they'd want to know how my talking-to-ghosts superpower worked, and whether I could sniff out any other bodies for them, and would I like to come and be an assistant detective at weekends with my own squad car. But instead they pretty much decided I was telling lies and kept trying to get me to tell them some other story instead. I thought about bursting into tears and getting them sacked for rudeness, but I couldn't be bothered.

Afterwards, the police went off and had a long

conversation with Andy and Chris. They sent me into the garden so I couldn't hear what they said, but I bet my new dads were telling the police I was crazy. They didn't want to talk to me again after that.

"Don't you want to interrogate me?" I said. "I don't mind. I'll be interrogated if you want. I could do you an Identikit picture of Amelia if you'd like. I know what she looks like. I could show you a picture. There's one at Jim's house."

"Olivia," said Andy. He put his hands on my shoulder. "Let them go now. They'll call us if they need anything more."

But they never did. You'd have thought they'd be *delighted* to find someone who could talk to murderers from beyond the grave. You'd have thought they'd be *interested* at least.

"Serve you right if you find lots more dead babies and don't know whodunnit," I muttered at the policewoman, when I saw her talking on TV.

But she didn't seem to care.

REMEMBERING THE DEAD

I thought everything would change once Amelia had gone. I thought . . . I dunno. I thought Jim would realize I'd been right about Amelia and tell me he wanted me to come back and live with him again. I thought I'd stop being frightened of everything. I thought I'd be able to sleep at night without nightmares.

But nothing changed. I still lived with Andy and Chris. I started secondary school in Bristol, which was big and horrible and confusing and miserable. I'm sure secondary school in Tollford would have been big and horrible and confusing and miserable too, but at least Daniel would have been there, and I bet the boys would still have played football at lunchtime. Growing up made me tired and depressed. The bigger you are, the less people care about you. They stop thinking you're cute, and start thinking you're a lost cause.

Grace got her A Level results in August. She got into the London School of Economics, which was apparently a pretty big deal. She and Maisy were moving to London in September. She'd been given a little flat with a bedroom for Maisy to sleep in, and Maisy had a place in a crèche for when Grace was being a student. I found all this out at a church service for the dead babies in Tollford. Andy and Chris took me.

The church in Tollford was full of people. It made me angry. Nobody cared about all the live kids in care who didn't have families, but they all came out for some babies who'd died years and years and years ago. I bet all those people would have said horrible things about the babies' mothers if they'd been alive a hundred years ago.

Jim was there with Daniel and Harriet and Grace and Maisy. I got all jumpity-jittery when I saw them. I thought for sure Grace would hate me after what I tried to do to Maisy.

"Let's go home," I said to Andy, but he put his arm around my shoulder and said, "It's OK, Olivia." And then Harriet saw us and ran across to say hello, and Jim and everyone else followed. Even Grace came over, although she hung back behind Jim. I could see her tense up all over, and I could smell her nervousness. I wanted to run away, but Andy's arm was round my shoulder, and everyone was looking at me.

In the month since I'd seen her, Maisy had learnt to

walk. She toddled right up to us. I started back, afraid. I wasn't supposed to be near her any more. Surely someone was going to yell at me if I touched her?

"It's all right, Olivia," said Chris. He picked up Maisy and lifted her into the air. "Hello, little girl! Hello, gorgeous!"

Then Jim was there, and there was a whole boring grown-up conversation about babies, and Maisy, and schools, and that's when Jim told us about Grace and the LSE. Andy and Chris asked all these questions about Grace's flat and the crèche. The flats were mostly for grown-up students with husbands and babies, which Andy seemed to think was awful.

"What a shame you aren't with the other first years," he said. "You'll miss out on so much."

I could see Grace getting pissed off with him.

"It is *not* a shame," she said. "I've been given *everything* I ever wanted. *And* Maisy. Maisy is *not* a shame, are you, Maisy?"

"Oh. . ." said Andy. "I didn't mean. . ."

Grace glared at him and I giggled. I liked Grace, I realized. I never thought I'd like so many people.

The service was dead boring. Hymns and prayers and readings out of the service book and the vicar boring on about evil. I spent it seeing how annoying I could be before Andy and Chris kicked me out. I wriggled. I poked Chris in the leg. I went, "I'm *bored*, I'm *bored*," and asked stupid questions like, "What are those numbers for?" and "Why has that vicar got white in his collar?" and "Are we *done* yet?" until Chris got fed up and sent me outside.

Outside was quiet and nice. Grace was sitting on the bench playing with Maisy. Maisy ran over to me again, and Grace came after her and picked her up.

"Don't you bloody *touch* her," she said, all fierce.

"I won't," I said. "I *won't*! Amelia's gone now."

"Huh." Grace didn't say anything for a while. Then she said, "Much good it does you, eh?"

I didn't know what to say.

"Maybe Jim will let me come back," I said. "Now you and Maisy aren't living there any more. He might."

"Maybe," said Grace. "I wouldn't count on it, though. If you go around trusting people, you'll always get hurt. Why should he care about you?"

When she said that, I just wanted to run away. Run far, far away and never come back. It's all very well not trusting anyone when you're eighteen and have your own flat in London. It's exhausting when you're eleven and a half, and don't have a mum or a dad, or even a home. I thought Grace was probably right, though.

"I wouldn't hurt Maisy now," I said to Grace. "Really, I wouldn't."

Grace shrugged. She was still all tense.

"I don't believe in promises," she said. "Any more than I believe in people. You've got to look after yourself in this world. No one else will."

Later, in the car home, I thought about what Grace had said. Was she right? I wasn't sure. Once upon a time, I'd

224

definitely have agreed with her. But now I thought about all the people I liked: Liz, and Hayley, and Daniel, and Harriet, and Maisy, and Grace, and Pork Scratchings, and the goats, and Jim. I still wasn't sure I could trust any of these people. But I *wanted* to trust them and that had to be worth something. Hadn't it?

SCOWLY CLOUDS

Liz came to visit. She came every week like she used to. I thought maybe she wouldn't after what I did to Grace, but she still did.

When Liz came to visit while I lived with Jim, I was mostly nice to her, but when she came to visit at Andy and Chris's I was horrible. I shouted at her, and threw things in her face, and called her all sorts of names. I thought after what I tried to do to Maisy, she'd finally have realized what sort of person I really was, but she didn't seem to have got it. Maybe she was stupider than I thought.

She took me for a walk in the park. It was wet and windy and muddy and cold, and although it wasn't actually raining, there were big scowly clouds looming miserably over everything.

"I wonder," she said, as we tramped through the

wet trees. I groaned. "I wonder if you're angry with me because you're ashamed of what happened to Grace. I wonder if you're ashamed because the placement broke down, and you're frightened that I'm going to be angry with you too."

"Leave me alone!" I said, but she wouldn't.

"I wonder if you know that I love you," she said. "And if you know how sad I am that you're so unhappy."

"I'm fed up with love," I said. "Nobody *ever* loved me."

"I do," said Liz. "And I don't think I'm the only one, either."

"Then *why* does everyone always leave me?" I said.

Liz didn't answer. I didn't really want her to. We tramped through the mud, and the brown-paper leaves which were beginning to fall from the trees. Tramp. Tramp. Tramp.

"Jim never wants to see me again," I said, looking at her out of the corner of my eye.

"Now, I *know* that's not true," said Liz.

I didn't answer.

"Have you told him how sorry you are?" said Liz. "Have you told him you want to try living with him again?"

But I shouldn't have to tell him that. He should know without me saying.

"He won't let me live there again," I said. "He'll say no. Because of Harriet."

"Well," said Liz, "that might happen. You need to be prepared for that to happen. But if he doesn't know that you want to try again, how can he decide if he's willing

to try too? You should tell him." I stopped walking.
I was almost crying. I turned away so that Liz wouldn't
see. She took my face in her hands and moved it towards
her own. Her hands were gentle, but her voice was firm.
"Tell him," she said.

MONDAY

I wrote him a letter.

Dear Jim, (I wrote)

I'm sorry for what I did to Grace. I did it because I thought it would make Amelia go away, but it was wrong, and I shouldn't have done it. I wouldn't do it again, I promise. If you let me come back and live with you, I will try really hard to be good. I will do everything Helen asks me to do, even if it's stupid. I will listen when you tell me things, and I will try not to be mean to Daniel and Harriet any more.

I hope you can forgive me for all the things I did. If you can't, I don't know what will happen to me.

I know I don't deserve a family, but I hope you will let me be part of yours anyway.

Yours faithfully,
Olivia Glass

I put the letter in an envelope, and Chris wrote the address on it and gave me a stamp.

"First class," I said. "It *has* to be first class."

"Olivia," said Chris, "you know this might not work, don't you? I know Jim cares about you very much, but . . . he has other kids he needs to think about. The answer might still be no. You need to be prepared for that."

"No!" I said. "It won't be no. It can't be!"

"Let's hope it's not," said Chris, but he sounded sad.

He gave me the envelope and I took it to the postbox at the end of the road.

"Number ten!" he said as I went, and I nodded.

"Number ten." I kept forgetting which one their house was. All the houses looked the same.

At the end of the street, a granddad was walking along with a kid a bit older than Maisy. The kid was bending down to stroke a cat.

"Puss!" he was saying. "Puss puss puss!"

"Gently," the granddad was saying. "Don't startle him."

Why didn't anyone ever love me like that?

The notice on the front of the postbox said the last collection was at 5.45, which meant my letter wouldn't be picked up until tomorrow morning. It would take all day to get to Jim's house, and there was no post on a Sunday. But it would get there on Monday morning. Perhaps I would know what the answer was on Monday afternoon.

Perhaps Andy would know when he came to pick me up from school.

"Monday," I said. I kissed the front of the envelope, for luck, and I pushed it through the letter hole before I could change my mind.

HISTORICAL NOTE

Amelia Dyer was a real person. She was born in 1837 and died in 1896, when she was hanged for murder at the end of a sensational trial. Nobody knows exactly how many people she killed in her long career, but it is estimated to be around four hundred. Some died at birth, delivered in such a way as to look like stillbirths. Some died of diseases relating to malnutrition and neglect while in her care. Others were strangled and dropped into the River Thames. It was partly due to the furore surrounding her trial and others like it that the care system as we know it was created.

Jim's house in *Close Your Pretty Eyes* is fictional, although Amelia Dyer did live in similar places, and moved frequently in her thirty-year career as a baby farmer. There is, however, no evidence that she ever returned to any of them after her death.

ACKNOWLEDGEMENTS

This novel had three editors: Marion Lloyd, Alice Swan and Genevieve Herr. You didn't always agree with each other, but between you you all made this a better book. Thank you. Thanks also to my agent, Jodie Marsh, and to everyone at Scholastic for your continued support of my odd book ideas.

When writing *Close Your Pretty Eyes*, I read a huge number of blogs and memoirs by adoptive parents, foster carers and foster care survivors. These were too numerous to mention here, but thank you all. Without your honesty and your bravery, this would have been a very different book.

Thanks to my fellow writers in coffee shops, Victoria Van Hyning and Tara Button, and my book-encouragers and moan-listeners, Susie Day, Pita Harris, Jo Cotterill,

Frances Hardinge, and all my online writer friends. Thanks to my lovely husband Tom Nicholls, for saying things like, "I don't mind if you don't earn much money," and "You want that printer fixed right now? Well, all right then." One day I really will start listening to your accounting advice. Promise.

Last but most definitely not least, thanks to Adele Geras for answering my panicked Twitter request for creepy lullabies with the most perfect of perfect titles. And to Phil Hoggart, who doesn't know it yet, but I stole his TARDIS air freshener to give to Liz. Sorry. I don't think she's going to give it back.